MARRIED TO THE DON OF NEW ORLEANS 3

MISS JAZZIE

Cole Hart
SIGNATURE NOVELS

Married To The Don Of New Orleans 3

Published in the United States of America.

Published by Cole Hart Signature, LLC.

Mailing List

To stay up to date on new releases, plus get information on contests, sneak peeks, and more,

Go To The Website Below...

www.colehartsignature.com

To all my bad bitches, I can see your halo.

ACKNOWLEDGMENTS

God, you really showing out in my life and I pray that you continue to. This has been a whirlwind for me. From having covid to hurricane Ida and losing everything, I am still living and have the ability to write books. Tell me that ain't God.

My mother, Cynthia, you the shit, woman. You never let my cape hang low. You are my number one fan and I'm glad you're my mother. Without you I am nothing.

My two divas on earth and my prince in heaven. Every late night, every book I release, and every hour I work, I do it for y'all. Janiya, Jacey, and (RIP) Damyia Jr., y'all are the other half of my heartbeat.

To every reader that read left a review and supported me, I love you, I love you, I love you, because without y'all I wouldn't be the writer I am today. I hope y'all enjoy this final ride with my Krewe because this book gave me the blues. ENJOY!

I
ZULU

Magnolia got hit with a small ass .22, but it was like six fucking times. The bullets weren't big, but they packed a lot of power. I saw the fucking smoke coming from the bullets that pierced his torso. A chill ran through me like it was one of my brothers on the fucking dock clinging to human living. The blood poured from the holes and seeped through his white t-shirt. I wish I could have plugged the holes with my fingers to stop the bleeding.

I knew I called Endymion, but I must have dropped my phone when I got up and ran toward Magnolia. I was in fucking shock. I took the gun from him, then his phone to call the ambulance. I knew KOE was about to be in full effect after this shit. Grela wasn't supposed to be out here. Strike one. That fuck nigga Nyx was in the wind. Strike two. Magnolia wasn't fucking Jahari. Strike three. Some stupid shit was happening, and the only nigga that could answer my questions was Endymion. I told them niggas to be on standby if shit went left, and I was fucking right.

"We're losing him, his pulse is getting slower, he's losing too much blood! We have to move him, now! Get to the trauma unit now before we lose him completely!" the paramedic shouted at me, breaking my thoughts. Shit was fucked up.

I had four of my hittas watching everything. Two snipers on the roof of the building and the other two seen and unseen. I knew where they were and that's what mattered, but where the fuck were their antennas when the fucking bullets started flying?

"Where the fuck y'all taking him?!" I yelled at the paramedics as I ran my hand across my beard.

"Dignity Health Center, we gotta go, now!" they shouted at the same time, pulling him on the gurney while performing CPR. I looked down at my blood-stained shirt.

"Pick up the phone, nigga! What the fuck is going on?!" blared through my phone that lay on the pavement. I hadn't realized I called Endymion until I heard his voice. I must have dropped my shit in shock. I turned around and noticed another ambulance trying to get Grela on a fucking gurney. I forgot all about that nigga yelling on the phone. All the noise around me silenced, and I had tunnel vision. All I saw was them motherfuckers trying to pump life back into this bitch and lost it. Where were the niggas that were with her? It had to be at least three or four of 'em. They vanished in thin air when they heard the sirens blaring. Scary motherfuckers. Magnolia's macho man ass didn't have nobody with him. I admired that shit though. On some one band, one sound shit.

"Let that bitch die!" I took off running in their direction toward the truck. I pulled the gun out that I took off of Magnolia and was ready to finish this bitch. Grela had already cost us so much with her lying and devious fucking ways. She didn't deserve to be saved.

I grabbed at the paramedics, trying to pull them from helping that hoe. She didn't deserve to fucking live. All the havoc and secrets she'd been bringing to the table was costing us all our fucking sanity. It was time to get rid of her snake ass. Khency would just have to understand. But knowing this cat ass bitch, she probably had nine lives and was only on number eight.

"Sir, please back up and put that gun away or we will call the police and have you arrested!" the male paramedic yelled as I watched the other perform CPR on this rat ass bitch. I was mentally praying she died because if not, she would be tortured later.

The word police made me stop in my tracks. I def didn't want to get caught up in Cali with the laws but the hatred I had for this bitch had me ready to risk it all. I had to back track and get rid of the keys of coke before the cops came asking dumb ass questions that I wasn't answering. I grabbed my phone and ran to Magnolia's Charger and hopped in the driver's seat. I said a quick prayer for Magnolia as I pulled off behind the ambulance and picked my phone up.

"Nigga, what the fuck is going on out there? Why the fuck we flying to California in the middle of the fucking night?! I heard you say Grela, the fuck she doing out there?! Speak, nigga!" Endymion roared like a fucking tiger through the phone speaker, spitting question after question. He wasn't giving me a fucking chance to answer.

"Stop with the fucking yelling, nigga, and I'll answer yo' questions. You know I can't handle that shit" I yelled into the phone, swerving through traffic. I had to keep up with the damn ambulance and this nigga hollin' in my ear wasn't making it any better. That yelling and cursing shit brought back bad memories when our father would holler and curse at me until I was blue in the face. That's why I was so calm now. Endymion made a nigga feel like a fucking kid being chastised by an abusive parent, and he knew that was a trigger for me. I got silent on the phone to gather my fucking thoughts because if not, I would crash and kill my fucking self. After a few minutes of silence, Nemesis was the first to speak.

"What's up, Zu, what's good? Tell a nigga what's going on around you. Tell us what happened from the beginning up until now." He knew how to handle shit without the yelling. Call it childish, I called it being fucking nice and treating me like a man.

"My bad, nigga, I'm just trying to see what's going on and why the fuck you in Cali. Haze let you leave?" That was Endymion trying to be nice.

I had been a little distant from Haze because this bitch Taishi was working my nerves. I blocked her ass and she still managed to get through. Calling me in the middle of the night from random numbers and shit. I wanted to tell Haze, but that shit would break her and I didn't want to be the reason behind it. I had to dead this bitch and quick. I wanted to get some of my girls I had on KOE to beat that bitch to death, but I wanted the luxury of witnessing her taking her last breath.

"I knew in my soul that some shit was gon' pop off at the dock in Cali, so I took four of my hittas and hopped on the plane. Two snipers and two invisible." I paused, trying to keep up with the ambulance. "Instead of Nyx showing up to meet Jahari, Grela showed up with hittas and Magnolia came solo. I couldn't hear what the fuck they were saying, but I know words were being passed because I saw their mouths moving. Then, Grela pulled her gun and bullets started flying. It was up from there. I tried to kill that bitch, but I was outnumbered and my snipers went after the niggas that were with Grela, but what the fuck I don't understand is why the fuck did Magnolia and Grela meet? What fucking part did I miss?" I barked in the phone, because I knew they knew something.

"If you would have fucking listened and stayed the fuck at home and stopped ignoring yo' girl, you wouldn't be in Cali in the first fucking place. It was a slight change of plans. Magnolia wanted to feel the nigga out first before the exchange, but clearly, his snake ass had other plans," Nemesis said, and I caught what he was saying. I fell silent.

"Yeah, nigga, we know you still running from Taishi, the fuck is you thinking?" Endymion said. I didn't feel like hearing that shit.

"What the fuck she got on you like that, nigga?" Nemesis asked me, and I remained silent.

"I took care of that shit with her husband. If that's why that hoe sticking around, she can go in the backyard too," Endymion said. I breathed a sigh of relief. That bitch thought she could hold me killing her husband over my head.

"Yo' scary ass about to lose yo' future wife behind a bitch that don't know how to stay in her lane. I don't give a fuck if she was kin to the fucking president, nigga, you come to me when you have a fucking problem. The fucking mayor could be buried in a fucking box too." I heard everything he was fucking saying, but we had more pressing issues at hand than what they were talking about. I ran my hands through my hair, exhausted.

"So y'all niggas mean to tell me that the leys are not in the trunk of the car that I'm driving?" I was even more mad because these niggas were laughing.

"And this nigga wonder why we don't let him handle no fucking drugs." Endymion laughed. "Nigga, that was a test run, test and run. Only instead, you intervened the test and fucking ran. You wasn't supposed to be out there," Nemesis said, laughing, further more pissing me off. Nemesis had this shit that he did with his voice that made a nigga feel like he was chastising a child, and it pissed me off.

"Nigga, Magnolia is clinging to life because of y'all dumb asses. Y'all forgot he had a wife and son back in Atlanta to get back home to." I was fucking livid that they thought this shit was funny.

"Nigga, Magnolia clinging to life is his fault because he wanted to get a feel for a nigga that wasn't even there. He acted on impulse because of some other shit I spoke with him about, and that wasn't the move," Dymi's mean ass boomed through the speaker.

"The fuck you told him like that?" I just had to know.

"Not on the phone, in person," Nemesis said, and I wanted to throw the phone out the car.

"Now we gotta clean up his fucking mess, so get ready to call his wife," he finished, and I let out a loud, exhausted sound as I pulled in behind the ambulance at Dignity Health Trauma Center. I could only hope that Magnolia made it out alive, or Endymion's backyard ain't gon' be able to hold all the bodies we 'bout to lay down.

2

HAILEAUX

I didn't know what was going on. Zulu had been acting so distant lately that after I took care of Dymi and nursed him back to health, I was ready to get back to my life. The life I had before I met Zulu's dust bucket ass in Walgreen's. I'd gone back to work. Khency and Jhenga begged me not to go back. Khency even tried to make up shit to extend my stay in the mansion, but I had no use there. They were with their men and I was alone. It killed me to smell him on our side and couldn't touch him. Shit was driving me insane and giving me toxic thoughts. If I didn't get out that house, I was going to kill Zulu in his sleep. To feel so close to a man spiritually and not physically was killing me. His scent was on his clothes, the sheets, my clothes, just in the fucking air, and I was suffocating. I needed to breathe, without him.

The days I'd spent in Endymion's beautiful mansion were nothing short of amazing because I was in my element. Taking care of people was my specialty. I enjoyed medically taking care of Endymion, but I craved my man. I only saw Zulu when he came in, took a shower, pecked my lips, and left back out. The shit became so routine that when he tried to peck my lips, it was my hand and his dumb ass didn't even notice. That nigga's head was on another planet, but I was about to show him what planet I was on. Sex was non-existent. Like, we weren't fucking, sucking, butt fucking, nothing. He barely touched me. If he had something heavy on his mind, he knew he could talk to me. Our line of communication was always open, so it had to that bitch.

I told Jhenga about it and she said he was on his period, literally. I laughed at her stupid ass because Zulu didn't have a fucking period. If Zulu was still fucking the build-a-body bitch or any other bitch, he had another thing coming. I looked down at my finger and my beautiful engagement ring sat there. I wanted to take the bitch off, but I wasn't. Maybe he was acting off emotion when he proposed. We might need this break to figure out what we really wanted to do, because this him avoiding me shit was about to get him fucked up. Jhenga said he wasn't fucking nobody else, but I begged to differ. If he wasn't giving another bitch his time, then what the fuck was he doing? I wanted to ask Endymion, but I knew he would lie for his fucking brother or tell me to ask Zulu, so that was out of the question.

I waited until everyone was asleep. I'd packed my bag and hid it that morning. Zulu was so out his fucking mind that he hadn't noticed. That nigga must have smelled a fucking rat because that morning, he came back early and laid across the bed. No shower or nothing, nigga was fully dressed. He tried to play sleep but I knew he wasn't. I felt him trying to secretly watch my every move. I did my daily routine and spent most of the day changing Endymion's bandages and keeping myself busy. After three hours of that, I walked back in the room to Zulu sitting on the edge of the bed with his elbows to his knees. I looked to his left and saw my Gucci duffle bag next to him. On the bed to his right was a .45. He was sitting there like a madman with his hair all over his head. He must have gotten in the shower, because he had on basketball shorts and a beater. I didn't quite understand the look he was giving me, and I really didn't give a fuck.

"What's up?" he said too calmly and grabbed the gun, pulling it closer to him. I was boiling with fucking anger because I knew he was about to play the victim.

"The sky, nigga." I smirked because I wasn't afraid of him or that fucking gun. I knew he wouldn't hurt me, so if that was his scare tactic, he failed miserably. I looked in his bloodshot eyes and knew he had been smoking or was tired. Fuck, maybe a little bit of both. I knew I pissed him off with my sarcasm. He got up into my personal space.

"What's with the fucking bag? You want me to put you in it? That's the only fucking way you leaving." I could smell the weed and liquor on his breath. He was stressing, and what broke my heart was that his heart couldn't bring his mouth to tell me what was going on. Gun in his hand, his face in mine nose to nose, I could see the weight of the world on his shoulders. If he didn't tell me what the fuck was up, how could I help him?

"No, you are not putting me in that bag because my clothes are in there. I'm going home. I see that I am no longer needed here. I gotta get back to my life," I told him calmly as I could. I wasn't backing down from his ass this time. Zulu was so fucking sexy, even when he was mad. His hair added to the thugged out nigga that he was as he towered over me.

"Ain't no fucking leaving, I told you that! The fuck part of that don't you understand?" He drilled his finger into the side of my head, and I smacked it away.

"I realize there are parts of you that you will never let me see, and I'm tired of begging you to let me in. I see you hurting, but you refuse to let me know what the fuck is going on, so I'm saving me. My heart is not safe with you, Zulu," I told him, and he threw the gun on the nightstand and tried to grab my waist.

"Don't fucking touch me, Zulu! You've been walking around this bitch mad at everybody for something nobody knows about, unless it's me. Am I the fucking problem?!" I didn't want the tears to come, but I couldn't help it. "For the past two weeks you walked around this bitch and acted like I didn't exist, so keep that same fucking energy, nigga!" I tried to walk past him, but he blocked my path. What he didn't know was that I was leaving one way or the other.

"You don't know what the fuck is going on, and it needs to stay that way," he told me, and I rolled my eyes.

"Why? Because you fucking said so? I am not your child, I am your woman, and if you can't see that, then you wearing the wrong fucking glasses. It seems like everybody around this motherfucker knows what's going on with you except me. We the only couple that's keeping fucking secrets!" I yelled at him. "Nah, let me take that back, you are keeping shit from me, so keep the shit. Pressure busts pipes, dumb ass! Let me know how that works out for you." I jerked out of his grasp, but that only made him grip me tighter. It felt like he was trying to break my fucking ribs. I grabbed the back of his hair because I knew he hated that shit, and he quickly let me go.

"Some shit just not meant to be spoken on, Haze." He backed away with his head down.

"And that same shit you not telling me is what's breaking my heart," I told him as the tears rolled down my cheeks.

Zulu grabbed my hand, pulling my body further into him. He had me contemplating if he really wanted to marry me or not. If he wasn't ready, he could tell me now to avoid further heartbreak down the line.

"Don't do that overthinking shit, it ain't what you thinking. Yes, I'm in love with you, and yes, I wanna marry you, but it's some shit I need to handle first." He pecked my lips with each word.

"What the fuck am I thinking since you think you know?" I asked him. If the wrong shit came out of his mouth, I was ready to throw hands with his ass.

"You think I'm cheating on you, and I'm not." He backed up when he saw me in fighting stance. "You wanna fight me, Haze? Like, you really wanna test my skills right now?" He walked up to me taking my fists in his hands. "Cut that shit out and stop playing with me. You know it's you and will always be you." He grabbed my hands, putting them behind my back.

We were standing in the middle of the floor, body to body. His face was so close to mine I could smell the vanilla shampoo that he washed his hair with. He brought his face to mine and attacked my lips, devouring my mouth. I didn't wanna moan, but my body betrayed me. My heart wanted to ignore the tingling sensation that my pussy felt as his entire head went to the crook of my neck and bit down a little hard then sucked to intensify the pleasure. He wouldn't let go of my wrist, too afraid that I would stop him, and he was right, I would.

"Mmmmm, Zulu," I moaned out loud as he French kissed my neck. His beard brushing against my skin made goose bumps. That moan made him let my hands go. I wrapped them around his neck, pulling him closer to me.

His hands went around my thick waist. My body gave in every time. I hated my body for giving in to his advances. This bitch didn't know how to cooperate with my mind. My heart ached for him, but my mind was pushing him away. His licked his way back to my mouth, sucking both of my lips at the same time, then the top and sucking harder on the bottom lip.

"You trying to leave me?" He pecked my lips then my neck while palming my ass cheeks. His hands were like an octopus as he rubbed, pinched, and grabbed all over my body. His hands were so fucking big that each cheek fit perfectly. Sometimes I wondered if he was really once a female. Bitches didn't have big hands, and his dick-to-hand ratio was big as fuck to be once a female. Did he have surgery on those big motherfuckers too?

"You already checked out on me mentally," I lowly whispered as my head fell back, moaning. This nigga and his soft ass lips had me about to nut in my panties. My hands cupped his face to try and make him stop, but that made him go harder. He was my favorite addiction, and a bitch was about to slip and overdose.

"I'm just handling business, I swear, Haze." He looked me in the eyes and picked me up, wrapping my legs around his waist. I saw the sincerity in his eyes, but that could be fucking lust because I was feigning for the dick. My kitty hadn't been stroked in almost two weeks, and she was leaking for him. I'd been yearning for this type of affection, let alone his dick being buried inside of me.

"What fuckin' business?" I asked him as I dry humped his middle. "You fucking that bitch, Zulu?" I moaned out, and he stopped kissing me to look into my eyes.

"The fuck are you talking about, Haze?" He looked at me like I was crazy. I went in to kiss him, but he dodged me and I kissed his cheek.

"You really think I'm fucking that bitch, huh?" His forehead wrinkled and his face turned into a scowl.

Yeah, he was handling business, handling that bitch's pussy was what he was doing. He must have forgot in the other book he came to the room smelling like a bitch and I almost fucked him up, but it's okay, I'mma let him have that.

"You tell me. You ain't fucking me, and I know how much you crave pussy," I told him, licking his neck. He moaned out.

"The only pussy I crave is yours," he moaned, but I didn't believe him. I was never a jealous bitch, just territorial. I never made a nigga feel like he had to be with me, but at least be honest, something niggas would never be.

Taishi was always at the forefront of my spirit because I knew how he once felt about her. I didn't give a fuck if this bitch cheated a million times or whatever she did to hurt his ass, I knew love when I saw it, and he was in love with her. I should have bust that bitch down when Jhenga gave me her info, but I was trying to be an adult about the shit because I had the nigga who owned her heart. Her fault, never mine. I didn't know what type of ties they had, but I was about to cut every string if they thought they were gonna play with me. One thing I didn't tolerate was disrespect. I gave him the option to leave me the fuck alone, but he chose to stay. The only way out was with a toe tag. I mended his broken heart. It took a while, but he was finally in Haze land, and I was loving it. I wanted to trust him with my whole heart but in the back of my mind, I knew that bitch was gon' be a problem. I hoped Zulu proved me wrong.

"Open them cheeks up and let Daddy in there," he moaned, fumbling with his belt. He fell back on the bed with me on top of him. He knew I liked riding his long, thick dick, but I had a trick for his ass. I was gon' ride his ass into a coma and dip out like I was never there. I didn't even give a fuck about the clothes, I just needed space to think and know if I really wanted to marry Zulu. He needed to choose me or the business that kept him from being with me at night. I promised myself that I would never mentally lose myself over a nigga, and I meant it. If it had anything to do with that bitch, they better run for cover, because I was killing them both and whoever stood in my way of that.

It had been a week since I fucked him silly and left. He called and texted at least 10 times a day. At first, it was the typical *you trippin'* or *I miss you*, then it quickly turned in to hate texts that consisted of *bitch you really left me*, *I better not catch you with another nigga*, and this was the kicker, *why the fuck you didn't leave the ring if you left me?* That shit was the funniest because he had to be a fucking fool if he thought I was giving him that ring back. I would pawn that bitch first for my pain and suffering.

Now here I am, sitting on a fucking plane, rocking back and forth like a crackhead, wondering what the fuck Zulu had gotten himself into that we had to fly to fucking Cali in the middle of the night to get his ass. I looked across from me at Jhenga, and she winked at me. I was pissed that I gave that bitch an extra key to my apartment. The shit was for emergencies only. I didn't consider Zulu to be one of them. Khency knew not to use hers because she knew not to come to me about Zulu once I told her I left. Jhenga knew too, but she was so fucking gone off of Nemesis that he had mind control over her stupid ass.

She came into my room all frantic and shit, talking 'bout Zulu was caught up in some shit and I needed to come, but I didn't give an ounce of a fuck. If he got into some shit, then he could get himself out of it. I didn't know about the shit she was talking about and couldn't care less. The only thing I heard was California. Then she went on to say that she thought I knew, but I told her I didn't.

Unlike Dymi and Nemesis, Zulu kept everything from me, and that shut her ass up. I put the cover back over my head, and that time it was Nemesis begging me to get dressed and come with them because Zulu was fucking up, and I was the only one that could calm him down. I begged to differ. Trying to gather myself, I got up and threw on a maxi dress with Gucci slides and left with them. No clothes or nothing, just me, my purse, and cellphone.

"Does he even know I'm coming?" I gritted, looking at all of them from left to right. Khency was about to speak, but Dymi grabbed her thigh and she sat back and closed her mouth.

"Does it really matter? You about to be my brother's wife, this is where you should be," Nemesis said, looking directly at me.

"If he wanted me there, I wouldn't be on this plane with y'all, I would have been riding shotgun," I retorted, and Dymi smirked.

"You're right. That nigga out of line for that. We didn't even know the nigga was in Cali until I got a phone call. I'mma fix that, though," Dymi said sincerely, and I believed him. Both brothers had been nothing but nice to me, so I had no reason to act crazy with them.

"What the fuck is going on that y'all not telling me? I know y'all know." My nerves were on edge and I was ready to go home.

"We don't fucking know, Haileaux! We came to get you so you wouldn't be left in the dark," Nemesis barked. "Zulu kept you in the dark long enough, but I ain't the nigga to do it. I'mma tell you the real." Jhenga tried to put her finger over his mouth, and he bit the shit out of it. She punched him, and I laughed.

"Some shit happened in Cali with Zulu. His stupid ass wasn't supposed to be there, but he's there. People were shot, some killed, but we won't know the rest until we get there," Nemesis said, not breaking eye contact with me.

That shit made my stomach cramp. Zulu always did stupid shit, but this was too much. I didn't even know how to take in the information that Nemesis just gave me. I didn't know what the fuck I was walking into, but what I did know was Zulu had some fucking explaining to do.

3
ENDYMION

I usually never regret the shit I did or said, but that sit-down I had with Magnolia was one of them. How the fuck did he know Grela was gon' show on the fucking dock instead of Nyx? I knew he had connections, but damn. I told that nigga to let me handle Grela and to not interfere. I had already spoken with Jahari and told him about the test run but clearly, Magnolia had different plans. I just hoped that shit didn't cost him his life.

"Why the fuck are we flying to California at 3 am, Endymion?!" Khency screamed in my left ear. My reflexes almost made me knock fire from her stupid ass.

"Because that's what the fuck I said we doing, you got a problem with that? Take it up with God." She stood like she was about to shake some shit, but I yanked her ass down.

"Naahh, sit the fuck down and don't try to show off in front ya la friends and get ya feelings hurt." She rolled her eyes, but y'all best believe her ass met that fucking seat. I saw Jhenga out the corner of my eye jump like she was about to pop her shit, but Nemesis patted the inside of her thigh and she calmed down. She knew not to get in our shit because when she and Nemesis went upside each other's head, I stayed in my lane.

Let me get back on track a lil' bit, before Zulu's extra sneaky ass went to Cali without my permission.

Before that phone call, we were at the house and Khency told me she was pregnant again, but it was too early because Potato wasn't even one, but I didn't give a fuck. Abortion was out of the question, so she never let that word leave her lips. I fucked her out her clothes, soul, and asshole before she drifted off to la la land.

I wasn't for her shit on this plane. I never laid hands on a female, but she was forcing a nigga's hand. At the house, she got a nigga good, though. My light-bright ass walked onto the plane with fresh scratches on my neck and arms from her evil ass. Don't get shit twisted, it was all hearts, stars, and clovers when she told me she was pregnant, but I didn't like the look on her face when she told me, and I knew she was about to say some shit that'd make a nigga wanna kill her. I wanted to make love and she wanted to fight.

As she swung on me, I kissed and sucked all over her neck and breasts until she smacked the fuck out of me. That was the second time she smacked me, and I yoked her ass up. When my hands made their way between her legs, her scratches turned into rubbing and caressing the same skin that bled because of her. She roughly grabbed my dreads as I fucked her in every inch of our bedroom until we crashed at about 1:45 am.

So y'all know hell opened its gates when I woke her up and told her to pack some shit for her and our baby boy so we could take flight. I wish I could have taken a picture of her face, because she was 38 hot with me. She said I should take Potato to Ms. Cyn, but I wasn't about to wake that lady up in the middle of the night to watch him. We were taking him with us. Besides, when we handled whatever went wrong, my family would be tucked away.

My heart skipped a few beats as I thought about the shit Grela kept doing to fuck up my trust. I blamed myself because I introduced my brothers to her. She was bringing too much heat to the Krewe and had to be eliminated. She had some hot lead to be pumped into her, and I was going to do it because she was my problem. I made a deal with the devil, and now I had to pay up, but Grela was gon' pay with her life.

Grela thought we needed saving and I let her in off the strength of us not having our parents around. She slithered her way into our lives and I was going to drag that bitch out. I had shit covered for me and my brothers. If anything, she threw Khency to the wolves the day she told me to save her from Kayku. Her blood would be on my hands. I brought her into our lives and I would definitely be the one to take her snake ass out. Lady Bug's hand on my knee stopped it from constantly shaking.

"Poppa, you shaking the plane," she tried to joke with me, but I wasn't feeling it. I hated that nickname she made up for me because she said I acted like an old man. She knew I hated that shit. The fuck was a Poppa? I ain't no old ass nigga.

My leg was shaking like a crackhead. My nerves were on edge because I was really lost. I was really about to kill my wife's mother for being a fucking snake. In the short time I'd been married to Khency, I had grown in love with her. I couldn't see my world without her in it. Her smell, touch, attitude, her body, even the way she slightly snored when she was tired calmed me.

Even her funky ass breath and crust in her eyes in the morning was a breath of fresh air to me. I would love her forever—fuck, she was my forever. I hadn't loved another woman since Jazz, and Khency came along and turned my heart into mush all over again. I didn't want her to resent me for killing her mother, but it had to be done. I'd spared her life too many times, and this was the last. Lady Bug didn't even know the entire story as to why we were flying to Cali in the wee hours of the morning.

"Whatever is going on, you gon' handle it, then we going home." She pushed against me and kissed my lips. Her voice was one of authority, making my dick brick up. I looked into her gray eyes and took in her beautiful skin and felt like the luckiest nigga alive to have her as my wife. I didn't deserve her. I tried to look away because my mind was all fucked up.

"When we get to Cali, shit gon'—" She shushed me with a kiss and a smile.

"Does this situation require me to be your wife or your lawyer? From the look in your eyes, it's probably fucking both." She looked from me to Nemesis, and he smiled, winking his eye.

"What I told you about that flirting shit, nigga? Don't make me fuck you up." I looked at Nemesis, and he laughed. Nemesis always did that to get under my skin, and it worked every time.

"You will always be my wife first. You'll know when it's time to be my lawyer, if ever." I pulled her chin to me and kissed her lips, sliding my tongue in her mouth. Khency was it for me, and as her maw clung to life, she'd better remain by my side. Fuck it, she didn't have a choice.

She leaned back, taking my bottom lip with her, and sucked harder. Her face flushed, a clear indication that I had her just how I wanted her, mind fucked, but not in a bad way. Her face always did this lil' shit where her nose crinkled up and her cheeks turned a deep purple. Her face displayed every emotion that her mouth couldn't speak. I told her about that shit, but she would always say I had her lost for words. We'd been together long enough for that shit to be a thing of the past. I guess it was out of her control.

I reached into my pocket and pulled out two boxes. I had my personal jeweler hook me up before all this shit happened. I opened my box and place the diamond-encrusted wedding band on my left ring finger. She noticed the other box and tried to grab it, but I yanked it back.

"I need to know that when the dust settles and shit goes left, that you'll still choose me." I looked at her with the ring in my hand. We were already married on paper, but we needed new rings.

"Why do you keep saying that, Poppa?" She grabbed my beard toward her face, running her hands through it. Khency was fucking beautiful. She was my dream girl. Shit was crazy that I didn't even notice it until this moment. She was so timid with a little hood in her. Educated with book and street smarts. She was a big steppa, and I wasn't about to let her go. If I had to hogtie her ass and drag her back to New Orleans, I would. We were locked in.

"Because I need to know that when sugar turns to shit because, I know it will, that you got me and will choose me." I looked at her sternly, and she moved away from me.

That shit hurt. My heart galloped like a stallion running on the track. My soul left my body. No other female made me feel shit like this just from a small gesture. It was foreign to me.

"Did I leave you yet?" She tilted her head to the side to look at me with a raised eyebrow. I loved her angry face. Shit was a turn on. Everything about my wife was a turn on.

"No, Lady Bug, but—" Her finger to my lips silenced my words. She grabbed the ring from my hand and slid it on her left finger and removed her finger from my lips.

"When I have nightmares, save me from the boogeyman, Endymion. When my nights won't turn to days, protect me from myself and protect our children." She rubbed her slightly poked out belly and looked back at Potato asleep in his car seat.

"Just love it all out of me because I'll always choose you, even if you're wrong, I'll choose you. Didn't I tell you that in book 2? What's changed? Different color, same gang." She kissed the ring on my finger as I did hers. That was our way to consummate our union. I don't know what I did to deserve her, but I thank God for sparing me to be a part of her world. I opened my mouth to be completely honest with her, but she stopped me.

"Tell me when we get back home." She pecked my lips and sat back because we were about to land in the sunny state of California for the second time with no peace.

4
KHENCY

Poppa must have thought I was stupid or dumb. I knew all about the shit Grela had going on, but I would let him do the honors. I knew back when she first came to me with the stupid shit about marrying Endymion that she had some shit up her sleeve, and I wanted no parts of it. Grela been a shiesty bitch since she met KOE. Shit, she thought I didn't know, I knew, but I kept quiet about it. I didn't even tell my husband because he would wanna fix it and I wanted to do this one on my own. Grela didn't deserve to live after the shit that was told to me. I couldn't believe she shot Magnolia behind some shit she did years ago. Jealousy would get a bitch killed, and she proved just what the fuck I said.

I loved Endymion with my whole heart. I knew he was going to kill my mother, and I didn't blame him. I wish the clip that Magnolia emptied into that bitch killed her, but in my heart I knew it didn't. The bitch had the heart of a lion, she wasn't dying yet. It would take more than a few bullets for her ass to die.

Once we touched down in Cali, we hopped in a car and went straight to the hospital. I hated them. When I had Khenzington, I had a water delivery with my midwife. The smell of death that loomed over hospitals made my ass itch.

I felt sorry for Haileaux because she didn't deserve the shit that Zulu was bringing to her doorstep. She signed up for it, but I was going to talk some sense into him when I saw him, because he needed his ass kicked for playing with my girl like that.

We walked in the hospital on some mob shit, dressed in all black. Even Potato had on an all-black onesie. Every Mason in California was there including Jahari and his wife. In my heart of hearts, I knew Nemesis had fucked Jhenga before, but they never let that shit out and I wasn't about to say shit because I didn't have any evidence. I held Endymion's hand tighter as I noticed Zulu slouched on the chair in the corner with his blood-stained shirt on. I looked back at Hails as she held clothes for him, and nodded for her to go to him. Every nigga's eyes in the room lifted as she strutted to him with her black maxi dress on, but she only had eyes for him.

"Did anybody call his wife yet?" I looked at Endymion for an answer because I didn't see her anywhere.

I knew her heart would be broken if something happened to him. My heart hurt for her because this shit should not have happened.

"What's the status?" Endymion said with authority to every nigga in the room. They looked at him before speaking.

"They still working on him. We haven't called Zenobia yet," one of those fine ass Italian men said. His accent alone made my panties wet. Endymion gave me a look of disdain as I walked away and sat down with our son.

I watched as Hails walked over to Zulu and stood in front of him. I couldn't tell if any words were spoken because her back was to me, blocking the view. Jhenga and Nemesis stood on the side of Endymion trying to figure out their next move.

"Oh, now you fucking concerned! Didn't you leave a nigga? Why the fuck y'all brought her here? Man, get this bitch away from me, NOW!" I heard Zulu yell as Hails stood there watching him, not saying a word.

"This nigga tripping," I heard Nemesis say as he began to walk over there.

She threw the clothes hard as fuck at him and walked away from him and out the double doors. Just before she got out, she turned to him.

"Get the fuck up and come on before I show my entire ass in front of people that I don't even fucking know," she yelled, but that nigga sat there with the clothes all over the top of his head. She turned her head a way that made her ass look demonic, because he hadn't moved yet. Jhenga pulled Nemesis back because we'd never witnessed Haileaux get this fucking mad.

"So, you not coming?" She looked at him with a deranged look on her face. He ain't say shit. Hails hated when a bitch or nigga ignored her. She spun around and damn near ran over to him.

She grabbed his hair in a vice grip and started to drag that nigga from his seat. I could tell Nemesis' stupid ass wanted to laugh but didn't want to embarrass his brother.

"Man, let my fucking hair go!" He twisted and turned his head like a child while she dragged him.

"Nah, you wanna act like a fucking child, so I'll treat you like one. You sitting here with all this fucking blood on your shirt in front of strangers. Get the fuck up, Zulu!" she barked at him as he tried to fight her. He was pulling at her short ass to let him go, but she didn't let go. She dragged his ass all the way to the parking lot.

After that fiasco, we walked over to Mahyesha, who was a ball of tears. I wrapped my arms around her, and she fell into my embrace.

"What are the doctors saying?" I whispered in her ear as Dymi stood beside me. I felt another set of arms and noticed it was Jhenga hugging her as well. We hugged and cried until they got it all out, and she pulled away from us.

"He's still in surgery. He got hit six times by that bitch you call momma, but I'm telling you, her inhaling then exhaling is fucking numbered. She will not take my fucking son from me. She already took y'all fucking daddy." She gave me one last hug and walked over to a chair and sat down. I noticed Endymion walking over to Jahari and headed that way. I noticed Jhenga lagged behind for whatever reason, but she stayed behind to tend to Mahyesha.

I looked around and it looked like the entire state of California was in attendance. They really loved my brother out here. Niggas was fine as fuck, but they knew not to even play the shit with me. I'm sure Magnolia already told him who I was. I saw a few eyes giving me the once over, but I wouldn't dare make eye contact with any of them. Once I made it to Endymion, I tucked myself in his side and he wrapped his arm possessively around my waist.

"What happened, Jay?" Dymi asked Jahari. Jahari looked at me with an exhausted breath then turned to my husband.

"I told that nigga to stay behind and that this shit was just to feel the new nigga out, but he wasn't feeling it. He told me about the conversation y'all had. It was like he felt that shit. He knew Grela was gon' be there and told me to stand down, and that's what the fuck I did. My brother never acts on impulse," Jahari said as I stepped around Endymion.

It was like he was noticing me for the first time. I was eavesdropping on their conversation, but Dymi knew I was behind him.

"Shit is all fucked up." I could hear the sorrow in Jahari's voice, so I walked over to him and wrapped him in my arms. I didn't think anything of it because he was my fucking brother.

"Girl, if you don't take your fucking hands off my husband," I heard behind me, and there was Amerika walking full speed toward us with a scowl on her face.

"Wooahhh, slow down, lil' momma, that's her brother, chill out," Endymion said before stopping her in her tracks.

"I know who the fuck she is, but I also know that the bitch

over there fucked my husband," she shouted and nodded her head toward Jhenga and Mahyesha.

"Girl, my friend don't want yo' fucking husband. Now ain't the fucking time for all that." I turned from Jahari, but he pinched my side to shush me. I was glad Dymi didn't notice because he would die ten fucking deaths.

"Aww, fuck, somebody gotta call Zenobia," Jahari said, ignoring his wife.

"Give me the phone, I'll make the call." Endymion finally found his fucking voice at the mention of Zenobia. Jahari tried to give him the phone, but I snatched in before Dymi could get to it.

"Nah, I'll make the call. Go find the fucking doctors for an update." I walked away from them to call Zenobia. He must have forgot how he was looking at that bitch when we were all in the bar before he knew her as Magnolia's wife. It was something about the fucking way he looked at her that I didn't like. Even after Magnolia told him of their union, he still looked at her like he wanted to devour her. I knew he told me she reminded him of his past love. Well, I'm his fucking future and if he wanted to stay married to me, then he might wanna chill the fuck out.

5
JHENGA

If it's one thing I knew about a hood bitch, it was they knew how to use reverse psychology like a motherfucker. Nah, this funny looking bitch Amerika gon' say I was fucking her husband when she knew damn well that wasn't the fucking case. I could bust that hoe's entire life open and tell her that it was Kizzy, but then it would look like some incest shit. I didn't need Dymi fucking shit up when Magnolia's life was on the line.

If she accused me of fucking her nigga, that meant she fucked mine. I didn't want the wheels in my head to start turning, so I tried to think about the present. Nemesis never gave me the indication or body language that he fucked this hoe, so I would stay in my lane, for now. Even as I looked at him from across the room, his demeanor remained stoic and void of emotion. He would have gotten defensive and wanted to kill this bitch if he fucked her. I couldn't worry myself with the dumb shit because my mind was elsewhere.

I walked over to Khency as she held the phone to her ear. We were surrounded by some boss ass niggas dressed in all black, and if I wasn't married, I'd bag a few of them niggas. If Amerika was here, why the fuck didn't she make the call to her friend? Let me mind the business that pays me.

"Hey Zenobia, it's me, Khency," I heard her say as I walked up to her. "There's been an accident in California with Magnolia," was all she said before the phone disconnected and Khency raised red eyes to me.

"She hung up, so I know she's on her way." Khency looked at me as I wrapped my arms around her as she wept. I knew she may not have known Magnolia for long, but that was still her fucking brother.

"Bitch, you see how big Magnolia is, that nigga gone push through. He still gotta get to know yo' disgusting ass, so you know he ain't going nowhere." I tried to make light of the situation and it worked, because she smiled.

"Did you see how Amerika was talking reckless talking 'bout you fucked Jahari? She way off with that shit." We laughed because I knew the real.

"That bitch probably fucked Nemesis before and mad because he got a wife now." Kizzy snickered, but it was probably true. The bitch was going too hard behind some shit that didn't even happen.

I watched Nemesis closely. I saw Amerika wink her fucking eye at him, but he didn't respond. That confirmed my suspicions, but I remained quiet. Nah, if the bitch wanted to be petty, I could fuck Jahari and have that bitch's head spinning. Put this pussy on him and have Amerika really hating me, but I wasn't built like that. My heart and pussy belonged to Nemesis, but if Amerika kept fucking testing me, I would share my pussy at least.

"That bitch keep testing me, but I'mma fuck her and Nemesis up," I told Kizzy as we sat down and let the niggas talk. Shit was about to get real soon if Magnolia didn't survive this hit.

6

ZENOBIA

I swear I didn't want a chapter in this book. I told Miss Jazzie to let sleeping dogs lie, but she had to bring me back in some way. I was cool hanging in the background being mentioned here and there, but when I got the phone call from Khency talking about an accident with Magnolia, I had to come in this bitch ten toes down. Y'all know the story of me and my baby from *A Nolia Boss Saved Me*, and while our story ended with us getting married and me being pregnant, Magnolia just couldn't stay out of people's fucking business. He had to have his nose in shit where it didn't belong. We'd made a good life here, just the three of us, but after he fucked me out my misery, he told me he had to make a run. I didn't think the shit would be all the way in California.

After that phone call, I packed me and Zeno an overnight bag and called one of Magnolia's bodyguards that he left behind to fuel the jet and have it ready. Anything else I needed there would have to be bought. I hated when he kept shit from me, and where the fuck were Jahari and Amerika? Probably already there, and that pissed me off even more because they should have called me and not Khency.

I knew she was his sister and all, but Jahari lived in California. For Khency to call me this shit had to be serious. I grabbed my baby .22 and stuck it in my purse. The bodyguard grabbed Zeno's carrier and we were out the door.

When we landed in Cali, there was a car waiting for us. I didn't have anyone to handle Zeno for me, so I told the driver to take me to my husband. After about a two-hour drive ,we pulled up in front of the trauma unit.

"What the fuck are we doing here?!" I yelled at the driver.

"This is where I was instructed to bring you and wait until you were ready to leave," he said nervously, probably because I yelled.

I grabbed the car seat and my purse and ran to the entrance of the hospital. I walked up the receptionist desk and she was playing on her fucking phone. I smacked that shit out her hand. I was waiting on this bitch to buck and I would blow her fucking head off.

"Where the fuck is my husband, bitch?!" I didn't give two fucks at this point.

"Zenobia," I heard my name being called, and it was Khency. She ran to me and hugged me, and I shrugged her off. Hugs and shit could come later. Right now, I needed to lay eyes on my fucking husband.

"No offense. I love the hugs and love, but where is Mahsyn?" I looked at her and she didn't answer me.

I walked past her and into the lobby, and everybody who was affiliated with Mahsyn and the Magnolia Masons were there dressed in all black, ready for whatever. The only fucking face that was missing was my fucking husband. This shit looked like something from fucking *Scarface* the way these niggas came to me like I was the fucking Queen of Sheba. One of them took the car seat then my purse, and Jahari and Endymion came to me to sit me down.

"No, I'd rather stand." I wasn't feeling this shit at all.

"Look, Magnolia was doing a test run and shit went left. He was hit six times and he's been in surgery for the last five hours."

My ears had to be fucking with me. Jahari was standing in front of me and Endymion and Khency were to each side of me. Magnolia had left the street shit alone. We were happy, and he was running his businesses back in Atlanta. We were good. Why the fuck was he hiding shit from me, and how could I not notice?

"Nah, he left that shit alone," Endymion said, as if reading my mind.

"We spoke on some shit that happened and he decided to act on it. For good reason, of course, but that wasn't the move," he said all nonchalantly, and I didn't want to hear that shit.

"Man, fuck all that, where the fuck is my husband?!" I hollered so loud the walls shook and the fucking world stopped. I didn't give a fuck about nothing else but him.

"Zee, he still in surgery, the doctor didn't come out yet." That was Jahari's stupid ass saying more shit that I didn't want to hear. If the fucking doctor didn't come out, why the fuck they didn't go in?

"All y'all big motherfuckers sitting in this lobby and you mean to tell me y'all didn't rush them motherfuckers and find my husband back there! Is he even fucking alive? Let me guess, Y'ALL DON'T FUCKING KNOW!" I yelled so much that Zeno started crying. Mahyesha moved toward him and picked him up to quiet him down.

"Babes, we gotta wait on the doctor." Amerika came and hugged me, and I broke down. My heart ached because I didn't know what was going on and nobody had no answers for me. I cried because I should have stopped him from leaving. He always told me where he was going and how long he would be. Whether it was to the store or just to take a walk. This time he didn't tell me shit. He side-tracked me with the dick and I was comatose when he slipped out the door. I was mad at myself for even being that fucking tired that I didn't feel him next to me or all over me.

"This shit is my fault. Had I not been begging for the dick he wouldn't have fucked me to sleep and left," I said into Amerika's neck as I cried.

"This ain't yo' fault, Nobby. Whether you were woke or asleep or even if y'all didn't fuck, he would have found a way to distract yo' ass and leave," Amerika said, crying with me. I felt arms wrap around me from behind and noticed it was Khency and cried harder. She looked just like Magnolia, the female version. Shit broke my heart. Then another female, I'm guessing Jhenga, came over, and I saw Amerika roll her eyes. I didn't know what the fuck that was about. I knew they had a fight in the last book, but I didn't know why. Amerika was very vague about the details, but I'd ask Jhenga myself later. We needed each other now more than ever because whether or not Amerika liked it, Khency was my sister-in-law and hers too.

"Enough of this. I need to speak with Endymion, because clearly my husband and him been keeping secrets." I let them go and made eye contact with Jahari and Endymion. I noticed Khency give me the side eye, but I ignored it. Nobody wanted his light-bright ass but her, and I didn't fuck around like that. Just as I was about to walk over to him, a scrawny, foreign-looking man with a white lab coat on came out.

"The family of Mahsyn Calvary," he stated, and we all looked his way.

"I'm his wife and this is his family." I looked around at everybody in the room.

"I'm Dr. Bradford, the surgeon that removed five of the six bullets that were lodged into your husband's body. I must say, he is a strong man. We had to heavily sedate him because he kept calling out for Zenobia." The doctor chuckled and continued, "We lost him twice on the table but were able to bring him back. We did have to put him on a vent so that his body can heal, so don't be alarmed by the machines when you enter the room. He can hear you, though. The last bullet that went through his abdominal cavity was lodged in his spine, causing paralysis from the waist down. With extensive therapy, he can walk again but for now, I can't remove that bullet. It may cause permanent damage. Long as it doesn't move, he'll be fine. Visitors can go in, only two at a time. Any questions?" the doctor said, removing his gloves and cleaning his hands with sanitizer.

I didn't hear shit past the words paralysis. My heart sank to my feet knowing that when Magnolia came out of this shit that he was going to be paralyzed. The fact that he wasn't going to be able to walk was going to drive him insane, but we'd cross that bridge when we got to it. I was just glad that he was still alive. If I could turn back the hands of time, I wouldn't have fallen asleep and this shit would not have been happening.

"Y'all go ahead. I'll be the last to visit him, but Endymion and Jahari, I need fucking answers, and now," I told them as everybody else waited for their time to visit.

I walked outside with them with Jhenga, Nemesis, and Khency in tow. When we got far enough from the hospital, Nemesis pulled a blunt out and lit it. They were passing the blunt around and tried to skip over me. I'd left Zeno with one of my most trusted bodyguards, so I knew he was good.

"Give me the blunt," I told Nemesis, and he passed it to me.

"What the fuck is going on? How did my husband end up with six holes in him and in the hospital? And don't leave shit out." I looked at all of them, and my eyes lingered on Endymion.

"Speak, Endymion, because I know you know," I told him, and I noticed Khency side eye me. I wasn't worried about her. I had a few words for her as well, but that's going to happen between me and her alone.

After he ran the entire story down to me, I was pissed. Not at them but at Mahsyn for doing that stupid shit. His gut never led him wrong, but he could have gotten to Grela another way.

"So where the fuck is Grela now?" I asked, and I passed the blunt.

"In ICU with her hittas surrounding her," Jahari spoke, "but the cops won't come. Them niggas got paid not to show up here." He saluted me, and I smiled. Jahari was always ten steps ahead of shit.

I didn't know what strain of weed this shit was, but I was high as fuck. We walked back in the hospital and it was my turn to see my husband. I walked ahead of them, which was a signal that I wanted to go alone. I walked into his room, and to see such a strong man look so weak and a machine breathing for him made my knees buckle.

"This can't be where our story ends. You can't leave me in this world alone. You know I can't live on this side of the earth without you." I carefully picked his hand up and put it to my belle. He didn't even know it, but I was pregnant. I never got to tell him about the baby because he left before I had the chance.

"You better stop acting crazy and come back to me, Magnolia. I won't live in this world without you. Blood in and blood out. Your words not mine, so you can't leave me here," I told him and kissed his lips, breathing tube and all.

"My son a fighter, girl, his tough ass ain't going nowhere long as you here," Mahyesha said as she walked through the door and closed it. I could hear the tears in her voice before I turned around to face her. She grabbed me in her arms and hugged me tighter, and I held her tighter.

"You know Mahsyn ain't going nowhere when you got my grandbaby growing inside you. This is just a minor setback for an even bigger comeback." We cried until she kissed him and we left out the room. I prayed to the heavens that God spared my husband, because I meant what I said. I couldn't live in this world without him.

7
ZULU

Haze was showing her entire ass in the hospital, but I couldn't blame her. She left a nigga, and the way I been moving, a nigga surprised she came to Cali. Taishi thought she had my life in the bag, but I was about to lay everything on the line to Haze in hopes that she still wanted to marry me. She'd gotten a room at Caesar's Palace and dragged me all the way to the penthouse by my hair. She knew I hated that shit, but I would never put my hands on her. People looked at us as she dragged me through the lobby to the elevators but didn't say shit. Once the elevator doors opened, she pushed me inside and hurried to close the door.

"What the fuck is up with you? Why you felt like you had to keep secrets from me? I'm about to be your wife, or was that shit fake too?" she rattled off question after question, not letting me say shit.

I fell against the wall and she walked into my personal space. Her face was so close to mine that with every word she said our lips touched. I tried to put my head down in shame, but she grabbed my beard to stop me from doing so.

"Nah, fuck the shame, it's just us in this elevator. What the fuck is up with you, Zulu? What puzzle are you trying to put together? Because, clearly, that shit ain't working. What are you keeping from me?" she said, staring in my eyes.

"Taishi got some shit over my head, and if I don't fuck with her I could go to jail. I'm talking 'bout football numbers," I told her, and she backed away from me, laughing. She laughed until tears formed in her fucking eyes. She was angry, and those were angry tears. I felt like my oxygen supply had been sucked out of me. My other half was missing. The other half of my heart left when she backed away from me.

"I knew that bitch was gon' be a problem, and what do we do with problems, Zulu?" She gave me a deranged look that I wasn't quite familiar with.

"We solve them." I gave her the same look she gave me.

"I want to know everything. Keeping secrets from me is what's gon' make me give this fucking ring back. I should not have to be dragged out my bed in the middle of the fucking night to fly to another state because my nigga done fucked some shit up and left me in the blind. Do you know how the fuck that felt that everybody at least had clue as to what was going on except me?" She mushed my head and it hit the wall. I balled my fist up at my side and looked at her.

"The fuck you gon' do? You breathing all hard and shit. You wanna catch these hands?" She turned to press the button and stopped the elevator. She was on one, but I wasn't about to entertain her with this dumb shit.

"Press the fucking button so we can get the fuck off this elevator, and I'll tell you anything you wanna know," I gritted, because I was claustrophobic like a motherfucker. My hands started to tremble as I rocked from left to right. She didn't know that. That was one of the layers that she had yet to pull off, but she was about to find out.

"Nah, we gon' talk right here and now since you felt the fucking need to be silent at the hospital. You had your ch—" She couldn't get her last word out before I pounced on her. I grabbed her neck, gripping tight as fuck, looking into her eyes. I had turned into the monster that I never wanted her to see.

"PRESS THE FUCKING BUTTON AND GET ME THE FUCK OUT THIS ELEVATOR, HAILEAUX, BEFORE I FUCKING KILL YOU." I jerked her head with each word like a rag doll. I watched the life slowly leave her body before I caught myself and let her go. Her face turned blue as she slid down the wall gasping for air. I watched her as she watched me with red eyes and tears rolling down her beautiful face. I ran my hands over my wild hair as I pressed the button to get us moving again.

She was frightened. Her face displayed fear. I never wanted her to be scared of me. In that moment, I was scared of my fucking self and of what I might do to her if we didn't get off this fucking elevator. I bent down to touch her and she jumped away from me. That fucked me up. The trust was gone. She looked at me like I was a stranger, and I didn't like that shit. With her knees to her chest, she was trembling now out of fear, fear that I would harm her, and I wouldn't. I loved her too much, but I couldn't be in a closed area like that for too long. It was my fault that I didn't tell her. I just kept fucking up.

When the doors opened, she was still sitting in the same spot in the corner with her eyes closed, scared to move. Her breathing went back to normal, but she wouldn't move. I was scared to go near her, so I kept the doors open until she felt comfortable to get up.

"I'm sorry, Haze." That came from my heart because I never wanted her to fear me. She didn't reply. I didn't want to leave her sitting there, so I walked over to her and lifted her up bridal style and took her to the penthouse. I noticed her dress was wet. She pissed on herself. I literally scared the piss out of her, and that fucked with my soul.

I carried her straight to the shower. I needed to show her how sorry I was. I turned the shower on with her still in my arms. I undressed her and put her hair in a bun then undressed myself. She remained quiet and looked at me. She wasn't mad, mad, but she was mad enough to do damage. I walked into the shower and sat on the bench. I tried to grab her to me, but she wouldn't budge. She stood there fine as fuck, just looking at me like I was the fucking scum under her shoes. I deserved that. Not only because of the shit I was about to tell her, but because I damn near killed her on the elevator.

"What have been keeping you from me? I asked already too many fucking times with no response, so keep that dick and your mouth until I get answers. Plus, what the fuck was that on the elevator?! You never put yo' hands on me, Zulu. Who got yo' mind fucked up like that?" She looked at me, trying to hold back tears. I wanted to comfort her, but she didn't want me touching her until I told her everything.

"I killed Taishi's husband. I never been a sloppy nigga but, I acted off emotions and killed that nigga in front of a lot of people." I paused, putting my head down and lifting it back up. "It ain't the people that witnessed the shit, it's her thinking that she got some shit over my head. Every time she call, I'm running for stupid shit. I never fucked her. She only gave me head. I only leave to not be disrespectful you because this bitch won't leave me alone. I block her and she calls from different numbers all fucking night, and I couldn't handle it. Then this shit with Grela." I took a breath and shook my head. "This bitch tried to kill Magnolia and set us up. We didn't know she would be at the port, but she took bullets as well," I told her everything there was to know. She just stood there looking at me with her hand on her hip.

"Say something, Haze, please," I begged her, damn near crying. She couldn't leave me.

"You got me out here looking stupid trying to save you and running into situations blind. Then you fucking with this bitch like she relevant when you could just kill this bitch and be done with it." She looked at me with tears running down her puffy cheeks.

"It's not that easy, Haze. She is related to the fucking mayor. We already killed his fucking son." I looked into her eyes.

"It is that fucking easy when a bitch becomes a problem to me. What the fuck that gotta do with me? If you want me to be your wife, then handle it, or I will. Stop fucking playing with me, Zulu. Had it been me with another nigga, you wouldn't hesitate to pump lead in a nigga, so I need that same energy this time around. I don't give a fuck if the bitch was related to Biden or Kamala. I want her dead, or I'll do the shit myself." The venom in her voice spoke volumes. "If I do it, shit gon' get messy, so take my advice and shut that bitch up permanently when we get back to New Orleans," she said and walked up and in between my legs. Little did she know that Taishi was in California. The bitch followed me and I saw her before we got in the car to come to the hotel. When Haileaux was close enough, I wrapped my arms around her waist, pulling her closer to me, but she didn't move.

"I'm not fucking playing with you, Zulu. If you wanna marry me, then get rid of your dead weight." She bent eye level with me and pecked my lips. I felt my dick jump. It had been a while since I felt her insides, and I silently prayed she was about to bless a nigga with some of that juicy fruit. She tried to pull back from me, but I pulled her to me by the back of her thighs between my legs.

"Don't fucking run from me," I told her as I grabbed one of the shower heads. I started with her head and let the water run down her naked body, giving myself a fucking show. My hand started from her cheek and glided down the outline of her body, and she shivered.

When her head fell back, my mouth attacked her nipples as the water poured over us like a fountain. Her hands grabbed my head and she moaned but didn't stop me.

"Mmmmmm, I missed this shit," she moaned as I kissed her belly button and pinched her lil' pouch that she hated. She grabbed the back of my head and put it right where she wanted it, to her pussy.

She backed up against the wall, leaving me to crawl to her, and I did. She was worth begging for, and she was mine.

"You've been a bad boy, Zubae." Oh, now she wanna fucking role play. A few minutes ago, she was pulling my hair out my fucking scalp, but fuck, I was feigning for the pussy, so if she wanted me to be a fucking dog, I'd start barking.

"I know, Haze, let a nigga make it up to you." Man, if my brothers saw the shit I was doing, they would laugh they asses off.

"Come here then." She used her index finger to beckon me to her. I crawled my ass to her until I was in front of her on my knees.

"Kiss here." She opened her pussy lips and her clit looked at me. I lifted one of her legs and put it over my shoulder and kissed then sucked her clit. Her shit tasted so good I lost myself and started going ape shit.

"Slow down, tiger, she ain't going nowhere," she teased as I hummed in her shit. She grabbed my ponytail and brought my face back to her opening.

"Make love to her. Show her you are worthy to be in her presence by kissing on her," she moaned as she controlled the pace. I flattened my tongue and slowly French kissed her clit and slid my tongue in her hole. Her hips did a slow wind on my tongue as I felt her clit swell. She got off on controlling me. It gave her a sense of power, so I let her have that. She mushed my face in her soaking wet pussy then pulled it away when I got carried away. That shit was driving us both crazy, because I knew she was on the brink of orgasm.

"Stop teasing a nigga and let me do me." I looked up at her, and she looked like she'd smoked 10 blunts when I knew she hadn't smoked one.

I stood up, taking control as I led her to the bench. She

probably thought I was about to let her ride this dick, but I wanted control, so that was a no-no.

"Bend that ass over," I told her, and she did, turning her arch into a perfect U. I slapped her ass, watching it jiggle as my head sat at her opening. She looked back at me and licked her lips, pushing her pussy against me, but I dodged it.

"Patience," I told her as I began to give her inch by inch of me.

"Fuck," I groaned because her walls had a vice grip on my shit and I wasn't even all the way in. I pushed in and hit the bottom, and her back arched deeper, giving me access to a spot I didn't know existed.

"Damn, Zubae, you found my spot." Her pussy got wetter and tighter. I was touching something but didn't know what. That shit made the tip of my dick sensitive as fuck. I picked up both her thick ass thighs and went in and out, sliding my dick to the tip because I didn't wanna bust too soon.

"I'mma fall." She held on to the back of the bench for dear life. I wasn't going to let her fall. I could carry all her weight if she would just trust me.

"You still leaving me?" I moaned, and I gripped her legs, sliding in and out of her at a slow pace. She didn't answer, so I stopped and let my dick sit inside of her. Her pussy muscles were contracting, so I knew she was about to nut. I pulled my shit all the way out of her. She turned her head around like the exorcist.

"Why the fuck did you stop?" She looked like a wounded puppy, but she didn't answer me, so I wasn't putting my dick inside her. I let her legs down and switched positions with me sitting on the bench. Control. Power. She had to have it.

"You think I should leave you, Zulu?" She straddled me, leaving my dick between us. She pulled the back of my head back, making me look at her. This shit was turning her on. I felt her juices running down my thighs.

"Fuck no. That shit would kill me." I grabbed the base of my dick and rubbed it up and down her slit. Pre-cum oozed from my tip because I wanted to feel her.

"You gon' stop keeping secrets from me?" she asked as she wrapped her arms around my neck and lifted up to sit on the head and bounce slowly. My head fell back because I just wanted to push her ass down and fuck the shit out of her, but she was in control. She grabbed each side of my neck in her palms, making me look at her. With both feet on either side of me, she teased me with her pussy.

"I promise I'll never keep anything from you, and that's on God," I moaned like a bitch, and she slid down to the base of my dick.

"Motherfucker," she moaned as she rode me in slow motion. I opened her ass cheeks to get as deep as I could while she bounced on my shit, taking me to heaven and hell. Her head fell back and I took advantage and sucked down the middle of her neck, making her bounce faster.

I slipped my arms under her legs and took control, bouncing her up and down on my dick until she screamed out.

"Zubaeee, pleaseeeeeesah," she begged, but I kept hitting her spot. Sex was our love language. We spoke with our bodies and spirits. My strokes told her what my mouth couldn't speak. She was my everything in human form. The perfect fit for me, and I could lose her behind secrets that didn't even belong to me.

"What you begging fa? Thought I would be the one begging." I stroked her until we got to the bed, and I laid her down without disconnecting us. I spread her legs wide with my palms on each foot and slow stroked her. Her legs trembled as I caressed the inside of her thighs.

"Zulu, please." Her eyes met mine in a lustful gaze. My hips rolled in a circle, and she looked like she was about to have a seizure. This pussy was too good to let it go.

"Why you trying to leave me, Haze? You know how many niggas want my spot? They trying to lose their life over you, because you are my life." I stroked her deep and hard. It was true. I saw niggas looking all the time, but they knew better than to fuck with what's already mine.

"I'm not, Zulu, oh my god, I'm not." Her head turned from side to side as I closed her legs and dove deeper. I felt my balls tingling and my toes became one with the carpet. My nut was rising, but I wanted her to nut first. I began to suck on her toes and she squirmed like a fish. I felt her walls contracting, sucking the nut out of my dick, and I fell between her legs. She wrapped her legs around my waist and kissed my forehead.

"Stop keeping shit from me or you gon' be next in Endymion's back yard." She hugged me tighter, and we both fell into a much-needed slumber.

8
ENDYMION

Six shots. All upper torso. No head shots. Grela was trying to make a statement. Those was her signature shots. She wanted Magnolia out of the picture, but not long term. Just to sit him down so she could step in, but she forgot how crazy Mahyesha was when you fucked with her sons, and trying to make us clash was out of the question.

Grela didn't realize that Magnolia and his crew and me and KOE did different shit. Magnolia was with that drug shit, but we sold guns. We would never clash, only make money together, so her little trick was gon' get her killed. I looked at Zenobia and almost forgot that I was fucking married. It wasn't some fatal attraction shit I was going to act on, but she reminded me so much of my ex love. From the wild hair that rested on top of her head to her small, dainty feet, she was the replica of Jazz. I think my mind was fucked up because the resemblance brought back too many memories, good and bad. It wasn't on no lustful shit. I ain't wanna fuck on her or nothing. Even if I wasn't married, I wouldn't fuck with Zenobia. Don't get shit twisted, I loved the fuck out of Lady Bug, but the sight of Zenobia did something to me. I watched from afar as the ladies all hugged Zenobia and showered her with love. That's why I became loyal to Magnolia, because she showed nothing but love.

Grela was a jealous being, attention seeker, would take any measure to make sure shit went her way, but not this time. I walked over to the rest of KOE and the Masons and shook my head.

"My apologies—" One of the ole school niggas stopped my words. I wanted to pull my gun, but I respected my elders.

"Grela has been a thorn in my fucking side for years. Fuck shit up then disappear like a ghost. Then she came across your crew and stayed." He started clapping his hands as followed by all his heavy hittas. Nigga would have thought I won a fucking Oscar in this bitch how they were clapping.

"You brought her to us and now we are indebted to you and your family. Magnolia will be fine. Allah has him covered," he said, grabbing my shoulder. I didn't know who the fuck this nigga was touching me and shit.

"What's yo' name, big homie?" I asked out of curiosity.

"Meyhani. Walk with me." It came out more as a demand, but I respected his gangsta. We walked down the hallway and got on the elevator, stopped at the fifth floor and got off. No conversation until we were close to a very quiet and secluded part. Two armed men stood outside of the door ready for whatever.

"It's because of you the bitch in there is clinging to life for killing my brother," he said, and the wheels in my head turned. This was Magnolia's uncle.

"I know all about Khency, your wife, being Mason's daughter. Grela's been after Mahyesha since she found out that Mason was never going to leave and eventually married Mahyesha. This beef shit stemmed back before Khency was even born and unfortunately, she's about to lose another parent. Grela was always a greedy bitch. She always wanted what she wanted." He chuckled. "Me and Mason took turns hitting that pussy, but I always strapped up. Mason never loved her and only gave her the rings to shut her up, but I told him that would bite him in the ass." He didn't have to finish because I knew the rest.

"The hittas that were with her out there, I hired them. They are Masons, but she didn't know. I also knew about Zulu and his snipers, but I knew she wasn't there to do damage because I told them not to," he told me we as we walked past his guards and into the room.

There lay Grela with tubes coming from every part of her fucking body. Somehow, some way, they saved this bitch. The machine rapidly pumped her heart and chest with oxygen, and my fist balled up. Meyhani looked at me.

"I spoke with the doctors. This bitch is suffering in silence. She is not brain dead, so she feels every bullet-piercing pain that my nephew shot through her ass. She just can't voice it. Imagine the excruciating pain this bitch is in and can't tell a soul. I told the doctors to stop giving this bitch pain meds, let her suffer for all the shit she's done. I've never been one to play God, but for the right price, a nigga would sell their soul. One word and I'll unhook this shit and she'll gasp for air, inflicting more pain." I could hear the hate in his voice.

"She slithered her daughter into this shit—" He cut my words off.

"I know, for you to take over the Mardi Gras Mafia," he finished my words for me.

"Yeah, but I kept telling her that I wasn't fucking with it. I had my own shit going," I told him as we walked out the hospital room. I didn't want to look at this bitch more than I had to. At one point I had love in my heart for her, but it ended when she thought I was her fucking pawn.

"Listen, son, your father, Adonis, was a Mason. What he did to y'all was fucked, but I stayed out of family business. You are one of us. You already own the fucking Mardi Gras Mafia. You and your brothers, but Grela wanted you to make her queen. That's why she came after you so hard. You have every right to pull the plug on that bitch, but you won't because of your wife.

Does Khency know about the shit Grela's been doing?" he asked, and I told him no. I was still fucked up off of the words he just spat to me. *King of the Mardi Gras Mafia.* I didn't dabble in drugs. It wasn't my thing. Shit got sloppy in the drug game. Too many chiefs and not enough Indians.

"I know you not fucking with the drug game, and that's where we have the team at. Magnolia don't either. Only if need be, but for the most part he runs his businesses in the A. You the plug, nigga. Don't nothing move until you okay it. I've been trailing you and your brothers for a while now, and it's time to take the throne. I'll be in touch, but remember..." He turned and looked at me.

"Your presence is always felt, never seen," we said at the same time, and he tilted his hat to me and walked away.

It took me a minute to gather my thoughts. I didn't ask for this shit. It made me hate my father even more. He was a part of some shit that my mother didn't even know about. My mind was spinning as I took the elevator back to the third floor where my wife was. Now was the time to sit and have a talk with her, because Grela had to fucking go. Soon as I stepped off the elevator, I ran into Mahyesha.

"I knew that bitch had something to do with my husband being killed and why my fucking son is laid up in a coma with bullet wounds in him. She was my roadie, my best fucking friend, but I never knew the larceny that bitch had in her heart for me. If you don't kill that bitch, I will. Tell yo' wife she can share me with her brothers," she said in the calmest way before walking off and out the double doors. I ran my hand over my dreads and walked toward the ladies. At the rate my life was going, I'mma have high blood pressure or a receding hair line before I make 35.

"What's wrong, Poppa?" Khency walked up to me, wrapping her arms around my waist. I didn't hear her until I saw her.

"Nothing, just thinking 'bout some shit." I hugged her back and kissed the top of her head. I was stressed as fuck.

My wife was a lawyer and I was a fucking king. I just learned a millisecond ago that I was about to be crowned the King of the Mardi Gras Mafia. Conflict of interest much? I felt her looking up at me, but I couldn't face her. Khency could read me like a book. She knew when shit bothered me or when shit was weighing heavy on my mind. That was the lawyer in her. She grabbed my chin, bringing my forehead to hers. Face to face. Chest to chest. I closed my eyes because I didn't want to look at her. She would figure me out like a chess game. My chest heaved up and down and my heart beat rapidly in my chest. I couldn't tell her the truth. At least not all of it.

"Open your eyes, babe." Her soft voice vibrated into my entire body. She calmed me, but yet I was hurting her and she didn't even know. My lids fluttered open to look at her.

"I heard the side comments and saw the daunting fucking looks. What did my mother do?" she asked me lowly but deadly. I grabbed her hand to drag her away from the crowd.

"Wait, hold up, I need to talk to you." I turned around and Zenobia was walking in my direction. I noticed the scowl on my wife's face and I tightened my grip on her hand.

I didn't know what it was about women. It's like they had his unspoken language that only they understood. We both turned around with Lady Bug standing possessively in front of me.

"I wanted to ask you about Grela and her connection with my husband." She placed her hand on her hip, shifting her body to the left.

"After I talk to my wife." I felt Lady Bug push back against my dick. I swear women were crazy. Khency felt threatened or intimidated when she had no reason to be. Zenobia stood there for a while before stomping off like a mad midget. I wanted to laugh, but now wasn't the time.

"Before you even say shit, either you want that bitch or she wants you. Tread tightly or you gon' be buried in your own back yard," Khency told me as she left me standing there scared as fuck.

9
NEMESIS

All this standing around shit was fine and dandy, but I was ready for that gun play. These niggas dressed in all black looking like ninjas and shit. I saw one of the old heads walk off with Endymion and wondered what that shit was about. He'd tell me later. I sat down in the chair and Jhenga walked up to me and sat on my lap.

"I don't trust Zenobia or her lil' friend," she whispered as she kissed my ear. She'd told me about the fight between her and Amerika, and I was wishing that she let the situation go, but knowing Jhenga, it was far from over.

"Did y'all kiss and make up in y'all lil' girl huddle?" I asked to be funny, and she mushed the side of my head.

"I'm here because my husband is here. I could fuck with Zenobia, but it's something about Amerika I can't fuck with. That bitch make my ass itch." I laughed because I felt the same way.

I prayed Jhenga didn't find out that I fucked Amerika years ago, because she would swear to God himself that it happened yesterday. Jhenga would beat the bitch up every time she saw her if I told her the truth.

"What is it about the girl you don't like?" I asked her, hoping she didn't spazz out. Today was a good day in the neighborhood, and I hoped she didn't act stupid in front of all these strangers.

"It's the way she looks at me. Then I caught the hoe looking at you like a piece of steak fresh off the fucking grill. I ain't like that shit," she said, eyeing the girl. I pulled her face to me.

"Fuck that girl. We not here for them, we here for Magnolia and his brother. You might just be seeing more of her. Shopping sprees and shit—" She cut my words off.

"We live in New Orleans. I don't need new friends, but looks like you made some." She waved her hand around the crowded lobby at them mafia-looking niggas. I had guns in every strap of my holster including my ankles, so if shit popped off, I was going out like Scarface, minus the coke.

I lifted her off my lap and walked over to some bulky, built ass nigga with a black trench coat on like it was below 0 degrees outside. He stood stoic, not even moving when I stood in front of him.

"What's good, how you know Magnolia?" I asked him.

"We his family," he and all the niggas in black said behind him, like they were the Mississippi Mass Choir singing a hymn. I looked at them niggas and wanted to laugh because the shit was comical.

I turned to see Zulu and Haze walking through the doors and bypassing Endymion and Kizzy. He looked totally different from when Haze dragged his stupid ass out of here with blood all over him. She must've put the pussy on him. I take that back. She had the look of the devil on her face, so they didn't make up.

"Let me holla at you," he said once he was close enough. Jhenga walked off to hug Haze, and I walked with Zulu.

"Niggaaa, what the fuck happened?" I asked him, and he ran the story down to me. I was in shock. I knew this nigga was slick but not this slick. I was pissed off because he didn't tell me what moves he was making. I knew he wouldn't tell that nigga Dymi, but me and Zulu were thick as thieves.

"Some shit just had to be done solo, but y'all could have told a nigga something." He looked at me, mad as fuck.

"Why the fuck y'all brought Haze out here anyway?" he asked me, and I frowned.

"Because yo' ass need to stop keeping secrets and shit from her, nigga. How the fuck you gon' know if she a rider or not? She needed to be here for your dumb ass," I gritted, because this nigga was serious.

"I don't get in yo' fucking business when you and Jhenga decide y'all not having a good day and she pounce on yo' ass, so don't fucking interfere in my shit," he barked, and I had to take a step back and really look at this nigga.

"Nigga, if you can't trust her, then why are you marrying her?" I asked him, because I needed the truth.

"That's a good fucking question. Ayo, Haileaux, come here for a minute," he shouted, and she looked at him and rolled her eyes. I didn't know what the fuck happened when they left, but shit wasn't good between them, or so I thought.

"Why are we getting married?" he asked her, and her eyes got big as saucers. She looked defeated and fed the fuck up.

"If you gotta ask that question, you bitch ass nigga, then maybe we don't need to get married." She took the ring off and threw it at him and walked away.

"You a bitch for that, Zulu." That was Jhenga's ass as she went behind Haze.

"Nigga, what the fuck is wrong with you? Why the fuck you did her like that in front all these fucking people?" I asked him in a harsh tone.

"She need to be on the next plane in the fucking air back to New Orleans! Who the fuck told y'all to bring her anyway? Y'all niggas must have forgotten she fucking left me. Ain't shit changed, but the pussy was good though." He licked his lips and smiled, and for the first time since he became a nigga, I didn't recognize the man before me.

"Laugh now, cry later, nigga, because when those tables flip the fuck over, you gon' wish she was by yo' side instead of the side of another nigga." I walked off from his stupid ass and went to find my wife. This nigga was off his rocker and on a path of self-destruction, but for what? Because the bitch who he looked up to as a mother was a snake? He didn't have to take shit out on Haze. He needed to take that shit up with Grela's snake ass.

I found them in the hallway with Haze crying her ass off on Jhenga. I wanted to interfere, but I let them have their moment. They needed this. Haze needed this. She was the more quiet of the trio, so I knew her feelings were hurt. I walked over to them and she looked at me.

"That nigga tripping off this shit with Grela, just ignore his ignorance." I was trying to save my brother from losing his lifeline, but from the look on her face, I was too late.

"Fuck Grela, and fuck yo' brother," she said through her tears, but I knew she didn't mean that shit. I gave her the ring that she threw at Zulu.

"You gon' need this. Zulu just in his feelings about Grela and taking it out on everybody in his path, so don't stress it," I told her, and she smiled.

"Looka my baby, being all sweet and shit." Jhenga walked over and pecked my lips. I needed to get a hold on Zulu before his ass barked up the wrong tree and got himself killed.

"He wants you on the first thing smoking back to New Orleans. That's not a bad idea because shit 'bout to shake this way." I looked at both of them seriously. That was the truth. A lot of bloodshed was about to happen, and I needed my most prized possession as far away as possible.

"After I talk to Endymion, all the ladies gonna lay low in English Turn until this shit blows over," I told them and walked off in search of Endymion. With them Masons on deck, Grela was 'bout to catch all this smoke, and I didn't want none of the ladies to become targets because of it.

10
KHENCY

Why the fuck I felt like I was in the twilight zone walking on the side of my husband? I kept looking at him until we made it to the parking lot. A million things were running through my mind that I couldn't keep up with. I may have been a little naïve, but I knew shit was all fucked up because my brother was in a fucking coma and Jahari was about to kill everything walking. I stopped in the middle and pulled Endymion with me.

"Nah, we ain't talking in private. What the fuck is going on, Endymion, and why did you walk away with that man?" I asked him as he turned to face me.

"Give me a kiss first." I looked at him sideways because I knew that was his way of not telling me shit.

"If I give you a kiss, will you tell me everything?" I flung my hair across my shoulder and rolled my eyes. He nodded his head up and down and wrapped me in his arms. His lips met mine as he deepened the kiss, and I sucked his tongue. I grabbed the back of his dreads and he palmed my ass, wrapping my legs around his waist. I knew he was trying to distract me, but it wouldn't work this time. I let my legs down and backed away from him, slightly out of breath.

"Talk," I told him and wiped the remnants of his kiss off my lips.

"Are you in love with me? I take our vows very serious, Khency." He called me by my government name. I wasn't Lady Bug or Kizzy, and I didn't like that.

"Yes, I am in love with you, and will always be, now tell me," I told him, losing patience.

"Do you trust me? Will you always choose me?" Here we go with this choosing him shit. I was over it and I wasn't repeating myself.

"I answered all those questions already and yet you still haven't answered the only question that I have for you," I told him, moving further away. I had a gut feeling that whatever he was about to say would change our lives forever.

"When I first met your mother, I knew I had a replacement until she told me about you. She showed me pictures of you and told me you were fucking with the mayor's son. She said she wanted him dead because he didn't deserve you." I thought back to when they came into my house and took Kayku. "Well, she wanted me to marry you to make shit look like Kayku ran out on you and the baby, so I stepped in. I didn't expect to fall in love with you, Khency, but I did." He put his head down then lifted it to look at me. "The mayor is on my payroll and has been for some years. Grela was fucking him and pumping him for information for years. She ordered the hit on Magnolia's mother and father." Now that took me for a loop because Mahyesha and Grela were friends.

"She had him killed because he promised to marry her when she had you but turned around and married Mahyesha and found Jahari. I got all this from the mayor, who is one of the founders of the Magnolia Masons. He stepped down to get into politics but always fucked Grela on the side, but that wasn't enough for Grela. She wanted more, so she created the Mardi Gras Mafia and wanted me to take over so she could reign as queen and dim your light. Let you sit pretty being my wife," he said, looking at me. I wanted to cry because my mother was a fucking fraud.

"How did she end up in this hospital, Poppa?" I tried to hold back my tears, but I couldn't control them as they fell down my cheeks.

"After the Weezy concert, we had a meeting and Grela brought some nigga named Nyx in to import heroin from Magnolia's ports in California. After the mayor told me all the shit Grela was doing, I flew to Cali on my own and told him everything. We both agreed to give the heroin a test run. Jahari would meet with Nyx instead of the connect, but Magnolia insisted on being there. Zulu's sneaky ass knew about the meet but not the switch up and went out there with a few hittas. Shit went left when Grela showed up and with Magnolia being there, and shots were fired. Yo' mother is a snake and is behind all the shit that's happening. Then, Meyhani came to me and said that the throne been mine for the taking. Grela was just trying to get in good with me to secure her spot," he told me and got quiet. I guess that was the end of his story.

"So, now you choose me because whether you do or not, Grela's hours are counted. She wasn't a good mother to you because she kept you in the dark about too much, Lady Bug, and now you don't know what to choose. Just trust your heart and I'll handle the rest," he said, and I didn't know how to feel. To know that my husband was going to kill my mother broke my heart, but she'd done so fucking much. I was numb. Everything in my life thus far was questionable. Even my marriage was in question. Did he marry me for my mother's sake, or did he really love me? I had so many questions, and the only person that could answer them was damn near dead.

"The Masons are our family. They admire my loyalty and I appreciate them for that. All those men in there are for protection, but I'll die before anything happens to you, and that's on God," he told me, pulling me to him as I cried. I hated my mother for the shit she did but loved her because without her, I wouldn't be here.

"So, you telling me that my mother is a target?" I asked him.

"For so many people. She has wronged so many families that she has to pay with her life. She is only still breathing because the Masons are trying to spare her for you. It's your call," he told me, and my knees buckled. I didn't want to choose my mother's destiny but if not, they were going to kill her anyway. I wiped my tears and put my big girl panties on. I hated to choose, but I had to choose the one who loved me.

That was a lot to just dump in my lap, but I asked for it and he delivered it on a silver platter. I felt vomit rise in my throat as I pushed him away and vomited the nothing I had in my stomach. For a minute, I forgot I was pregnant and this all-day sickness was kicking my ass.

"Let me be the one to do it. After all, it's a life for a life, right?" I told him as I rubbed my not protruding belly, leaning my forehead to his.

11

ENDYMION

2 WEEKS AND SOME NICKELS LATER

Two weeks had passed and Magnolia was still in a coma, and we were still mobbing deep in Cali. Everybody was staying at the beach house on the outskirts of LA. The good thing was that Magnolia was off the breathing tube and had a nasal cannula in his nose, and we were just waiting on him to wake up. He was gonna shut down when they told him he would be paralyzed from the waist down, but with therapy he would be fine. I'd sent Khency, Jhenga, and Haze back to New Orleans until we had this shit figured out. Zenobia and Amerika were taking turns around the clock sitting with Magnolia while we plotted at the house. We didn't know who was for us and who was against us. Everybody was strapped when they left the house, and the ladies had bodyguards with them everywhere they went. Grela was still clinging to life until we decided what the move was. Zulu was moving reckless as fuck, and I needed to talk to him before he got himself killed.

I walked straight to his room and slammed the door. He pulled his gun out and aimed it at me.

"You can trust every nigga in here, put that gun away," I told him, and he put it down and sat on the bed.

"What's up with you and Haze? Nemesis told me how you treated her," I told him straight up.

"This shit with Taishi fucking with me. I wish I could just kill this bitch and be done with it. She just won't go away. I'll let Haze go before I hurt her," he said with a sad look in his eyes.

"You still got eyes on her?" I asked him.

"Yeah, that bitch in New Orleans. I don't need her running into Haze on no dumb shit," he told me, and I nodded my head.

"Haze can handle herself. Give the girl some credit. She got some dogs on her. She looked like it from the way she dragged yo' ass out the hospital," I told him, and it was the truth. Haze was a silent killer.

"Taishi ain't making no noise. She just don't want me happy. If she had me, she wouldn't want me anyway. She just don't want me with Haze," he told me, and it made sense. But what I didn't understand was why he didn't kill this bitch yet. Zulu's trigger finger was always itching.

"Well, what's the move then? You gon' let this bitch run yo' life from afar?" I asked him, because he looked stressed. Nigga looked like he even lost a little weight. This shit was bigger than Taishi and Haze, though. It was Grela.

"Speak, nigga," I told him.

"I can't believe I trusted Grela, man. She really treated me like I was her son." He put his head down, and I felt that shit.

"Nigga, how the fuck you think I feel? She loved on us like Momma did, only to be a wolf in sheep's clothing. To know I gotta kill my wife's mother has been taunting me since Meyhani spoke it," I told him.

"She was trying to secure her spot as queen when we don't need one because we are the three kings," I told him and broke everything down to him concerning the mafia shit.

"But we don't handle drugs, man. I ain't fucking with it," he said, and I agreed.

"We got a team for that, nigga. We just sit back and oversee everything. Order the hits and never get our hands dirty, like always," I told him, and he smiled. This nigga loved having power, so I knew he would love this shit.

"What about Khency?" he asked me.

"She knows and also knows I'll protect her and her career. The less she knows the less she'll be able to tell if shit goes left, but it won't," I assured him, and he nodded his head.

"Make up with ya girl for another take yo' spot, nigga." I got up and went back to my room.

I sat on my bed and grabbed my phone. I Facetimed Khency to see what her and her son were doing. I felt incomplete without them here with me. She answered on the first ring. I smiled when her face appeared on the screen.

"I miss yo' pretty ass," I told her, and she blushed. She looked like she only had on a bra because the upper half of her body was free of clothes.

"Where my son? Yo' ass half-naked." She chuckled, and I saw she picked up a wine glass and began to drink.

"He sleep and I'm having a drink," she said, sticking her tongue out at me. Shit made my dick hard.

"I miss you, Poppa, how much longer?" Her voice was sultry, making me miss her even more. She had her hair all over her face. I could tell she was tipsy. Her gray eyes were low like she smoked a blunt.

"Let Poppa see that pussy," I told her with my hand in my joggers.

"You want me to play in it?" she asked, putting the phone down, I'm guessing to grab something. When she popped back up on the screen, she had a little toy shit that looked like a rose with her ring light between her legs.

She laid back on the bed with her hair sprawled all over the pillow, and I imagined myself there with her. She lifted up and took her panties off and spread her legs so I could see her entire pussy. She turned the toy on and aimed it straight for her clit and began rubbing it. Her other hand pulled her bra cup to the side and pinched her nipples. I stroked my dick as I watched her pleasure herself and moan my name loud as fuck. I had to turn the volume down on my phone so no one would hear her.

"Damn, twist that bitch just like that" I told her, and she opened her legs wider to give me a better view. I saw her clit jumping and felt my nut rising to the tip of my dick.

"Ummmm, Poppa, kiss this pussy." My mouth salivated like a dog as I watched her hairless pussy get wetter and wetter.

"Fuck, Khency, you gon' make me bust, baby," I told her and stroked my meat faster and faster. I put the phone against the pillows I had propped up so I could put my other hand on the back of my head, gripping my shit as I looked closer at the screen.

"Oh shit, Endymion, I'm 'bout to come, baby," she moaned as I witnessed nut squirt out her pussy and run down her ass crack. Just seeing that shit made me nut in my hands. Her hands made their way to her pussy, and she slid nut on her finger and sucked it off her fingers. My nut shot out my dick like a missile looking at that shit.

"You tryna kill a nigga with that shit," I told her, and she looked like she was about to pass out from the orgasm. She sat up and put her face back in the camera.

"I needed that because I missed that dick." She giggled like a school girl as I took her in. I looked at every inch of her face, and I knew I'd risk it all to be with her.

"I miss you and my son plus one," I told her, speaking of the baby in her belly. I couldn't wait for her to get fat and eat everything in sight.

"Wait, that was red wine, right?" I fussed, because I didn't want my baby to be drunk in the womb.

"Duh, silly, of course. This is the only thing that seems to stay in my stomach. I think this baby an alcoholic." She laughed with lazy eyes.

"Well, get some rest. I know you probably got cases out the ass," I told her as she cleaned herself and got comfortable in our bed.

"Yeah, but I'm working from home and the girls are down the hall just in case Potato wakes up," she told me as her eyes began to close.

"Go head, baby momma, go to sleep and I'll call you in the morning. Give me kiss," I told her, and she put her face close to the phone. She gave me air kisses and we disconnected the call. These niggas needed to make up their mind about what they were gonna do with this bitch, because I was starting to miss my wife and family a little too much. They had one week to decide what the fuck they were gonna do, or I was leaving. All they had to do was pull the plug on this bitch and let her go, but them prolonging shit was pissing me off.

The Masons were worldwide, so why we were out here, the others were handling business and getting shit together for me to take over. I was ready to be done with this shit, but I had to have patience when dealing with these niggas, I see.

After I showered, I went to the kitchen to find something to eat and found Mahyesha fixing dinner.

"I know you back there. My reflexes are sharp as a tack, have a seat." She pointed to the seat on the island.

"Before you say anything, let me speak," she said, stirring the pot of spaghetti.

"Grela and I were best friends, but I always felt the bitch was jealous of me and Big Mason. When I found out he was fucking her, I didn't care because one turned into three. All three of us were in the relationship. What they call it, poly?" She laughed as she reflected.

"That shit been around for years. It's just not a secret in y'all generation. Mason was tired of the three-way relationship. He wanted a family. But with me only. I don't know what the fuck he told that bitch, but she disappeared like a ghost. Magnolia was three. I later found out the bitch was pregnant, but by then she had cut all ties with me. Mason knew about Khency, but Grela just didn't want her around us.

"Something in her spirit changed. She became evil. I soon

ignored the harassing phone calls, breaking car windows, and flatting tires until it eventually stopped and so did our friendship." She sniffed but continued, "I never thought she would go to great lengths to hurt us. When Magnolia told me about the hit she put on my husband, I was hurt. She wanted me to suffer for the rest of my life. I gave her that control for a while until I realized all I had to do was forgive her to get my power back. I forgave her, but she never forgave me."

She stopped and turned to me. "Go in the fridge and reach me that cheese." I did what she said, and she kept talking. "Khency don't deserve a mother like that. She kept that child from all the evil she put in the universe. At least she did something right. I always wanted a daughter and from the looks of it, I'll finally get one, because Grela gon' die tonight, nah set the table." She didn't say no more, and I didn't have a response. I learned from Magnolia that Mahyesha's word was law, and who was I to judge when we wanted to same thing, just at the expense of hurting my wife.

12

HAILEAUX

I was depressed. The not eating, losing weight, and couldn't function depressed. Zulu was one confused motherfucker, and I was over the dumb shit. He wanted to play games, well let the games begin, but I promise y'all he won't win. I was the queen of playing games, and I could make that nigga wanna kill me. When we first got back to New Orleans, everybody went back to their daily routine. Khency was still working from home because of the baby, and Jhenga was back working at her shop with bodyguards, of course. But I just couldn't pull myself together to go to work. I wasn't hurting for money, so I could sleep in a few days, and that's exactly what I did. I locked myself in the room and didn't come out. I needed this, though. I'd lost myself loving Zulu, and all he did was break my fucking heart again.

After he made me show my ass and made love to me, begging me to stay with him, he started acting crazy at the hospital. I started not to put my ring back on, but fuck it, it was mine. This nigga went through all that at the concert to second guess me? I didn't think so. I was his only choice, and he was about to see just what the fuck I meant.

I hadn't bathed in three days. I didn't know if I was coming or going, but all that moping and being fucking stank stopped today. It was Friday and I wanted a drink. I knew Jhenga would be tired and Khency would have the baby, and plus she was pregnant, so I decided to go out alone. I needed this peace, and being cooped up in this room waiting on a phone call from his dog ass wasn't gon' help. I needed music and drinks in my system.

I got up showered and washed my hair, putting it in a bun. I was glad I stopped at home after the plane ride and got me some cute clothes from home. I pulled out red bodycon dress with my red and white Jordans, threw on a pair of large hoop earrings and matte red lipstick. I was making a statement tonight that I was sure to hear about tomorrow. I snapped a couple of pics for the gram, even did a boomerang to post later because I knew Zulu would be stalking my page. I was a big steppa tonight and all bets were off. I stepped out the door and ran into Jhenga. I rolled my eyes as she looked me up and down.

"Who you tryna cheat on my brother with? All yo' ass and titties and shit out, but you cute though," she told me and started laughing. "Bitch, Zulu gon' kill you." I laughed this time because she had no idea of the shit I was about to get into.

"Even the devil wore red, bitch, don't wait up." I grabbed the keys to her Camaro and left out the door on my way to the Hangover Bar.

It took me about 20 minutes to get there and find a parking spot, and it was lit. The line was wrapped around the corner but, of course, I paid a hundred dollars to bypass the line. I came out this way because I knew nobody would see me and tell Zulu, not that I cared any fucking way. I made my way to the bar and ordered two shots of Henny, because y'all know brown make you clown. I ordered a long island tea and found me a table not too far from the dance floor. Niggas were looking but were too scared to approach me. Probably because they knew I fucked with Zulu. Either way, I wasn't tripping. I was sipping on my drink until the DJ dropped my shit.

Why you be givin' up on us?
Like you don't know all the shit we been through
Everything used to be right, now you be actin' brand new
Thought that I was your friend too
If we in it, it's gonna take two
I be yellin' until I go blue, but I never would give up on you
And fuck everybody that's hatin'
Degrading they always got something to say
The wanna see us apart, that's why they smile in your face
Tatted your name on my heart, that way it never would fade
Even when loving get hard, you somebody I never would trade
You're somebody I'll never forget
'Cause with you all my feelings legit
These oth-er couples ain't on shit
No one else in my heart is gon' fit
I want you to be there when I'm rich
And I know that I act like a bitch
But, you should just make me yo' miss
If we fall, we just taking a risk

Dreezy's "Up and Down" boomed through the speakers, and I got up, drink in hand, and went to the dance floor. I was feeling my drink and the effects of the blunt I faced in the car. I swayed my hips from left to right, keeping up with the beat with my hands. I needed this. This alone time to figure out what the fuck Zulu was gon' do with our life. I loved him, but clearly love wasn't enough. Hands in the air, I slow winded. Thinking about Zulu's dick inside of made me go harder, until I felt a pair of arms wrapped around my waist and I froze.

I turned around to see a caramel-colored ass nigga. I'm talking 'bout the caramel that be inside the fucking Snickers bar. He smiled and the bottom platinum on his fangs made my pussy purr. His dreads hung over his face, touching my skin. That's how close he was. His hands never left my hips until I backed away, but he pulled me closer. Fuck it, I was single for the night anyway. He had to be at least 6'2 because he towered over me. I pulled his hair back from his face and recognized him as the nigga that Grela brought to the last meeting I walked in on.

"Nyx, is it?" I asked him above the music.

"You know who I am, so stop playing." He chuckled, and even that shit turned me on. "Zulu let you out to play tonight? He shouldn't have done that," he said so close to my lips that they almost touched. My breath hitched in my throat, but I remained cool.

"I'm not a dog, so he didn't let me do anything," I told him, never moving out his face.

"His fuck up not mine, beautiful." His hand was in my curls as the DJ slowed the music down and dropped Silk's "Lose Control."

Baby won't you let me look inside your soul
Let me make you lose control
Let me be the one you need
Baby just come to me
Now tell me girl what you want from me
Whatever it is you desire
I want to give my baby
I want to feel your body yearn
All your softest spots I plan to learn
Baby won't you let me just kiss you down
Make you spin around and 'round
Flip you girl from left to right
If you don't mind
Baby can I just spend the night

Nyx sang in my ear, and I melted. His big hands caressed my back, massaging all my tension away. This nigga was dangerous, and I couldn't cheat with him knowing he didn't fuck with my nigga. But I couldn't lie and say his touch wasn't mesmerizing and hypnotizing. We swayed to the beat until he turned me back around with my back to his chest and held me tight. I felt his hard dick against my ass and moved harder against it.

"You trying to get me in trouble," I whispered as his head was in the crook of my neck, kissing and licking my earlobe.

"You getting yo'self in trouble fucking with me," he whispered back, letting his hands glide down the front of my dress. I was so glad the lights were dim as his hand made its way up the front of my dress to my shaved pussy.

"Let me make you lose control, just one night, our secret." That shit sounded good, but I loved Zulu. The way Nyx's fingers strategically circled my clit made my knees buckle.

"You got a nigga begging you to lay you down, love. I ain't never had to beg for pussy," he moaned, sliding his finger inside of me, and I moaned. This nigga had my body on fire, and I liked it. Sweat grew on top of my lips, and he wiped it with his free hand. The baritone in his voice was one of need, craving, yearning. Like he needed me to put him out his misery. He wanted this pussy, was damn near begging for it, and I was about to give it to him.

I turned around, and I heard a bitch's voice. I was caught off guard as I watched this bitch Taishi walk past me with her girls and say, "And he think he got an angel and this bitch sleeping with the devil. Perfect Patty ain't so perfect, huh." She chuckled and her girls laughed.

I had had enough of this bitch playing with me. I was really mad because the bitch caught me red handed, and I didn't need her to have something to hold over my head. Something to run back and tell Zulu about his bitch damn near fucking the enemy in the club. I snatched away from Nyx and followed her to the bathroom. I didn't need my girls with me this time. This was my battle, and I was choosing it. I heard Nyx calling my name, but I had tunnel vision. All I heard and saw was this bitch going to the bathroom and her words taunting me.

I busted in the bathroom, and this bitch was in the mirror

acting like she was fixing her makeup. Her girls made a protective circle around her, but I didn't give a fuck.

"Bitch, you ain't that stupid to come in this bitch without ya girls. Clearly you outnumbered, so back the fuck up," was all she got out before I rushed her stupid ass.

I grabbed her by the face using my right hand and stung that bitch's face with my left fist. All face shots. No pulling hair and no scratching, because I wasn't a fucking cat. This fight was a long time coming. I took all my anger, frustration, and emotions out on this bitch. If her girls jumped in, I didn't feel a lick because I was focused on this bitch and her playing with me and my nigga. I didn't give a fuck if they recorded this shit. I was tired of her having something to hold over my nigga's head. I plummeted her head with my fist. Blood flew from her mouth along with a few teeth, and that shit went on my dress, and that infuriated me more. I stood to my feet and dragged her to the mirror and bashed her head into it. I felt somebody hit me in the back of the head with a bottle. I got stuck for a minute, but that didn't stop me from bashing Taishi's head into the mirror. Bitch was bloody and barely conscious.

Blocka Blocka

I heard gunshots and stopped instantly, leaving that hoe leaking in the sink. I felt an arm around my waist securely pulling me from the bathroom.

"Back the fuck up before I air this bitch out," I heard Nyx behind me as he dragged me to the nearest exit. The adrenaline I once had left, and regret sank in. I think I killed the bitch. My body trembled, and he lifted me up and threw me over his shoulder and walked to the parking lot. I let my anger get the best of me, and I hadn't done that shit in years.

Nyx opened the door to his car and put me in the passenger seat. Then I thought about Jhenga's car.

"Wait, I drove here. I can't leave my girl's car here," I told Nyx as he went to close the door.

"Let me take a look at that gash on the back of your head for you, then I'll bring you back to yo' car." Then it dawned on me that I could take care of my fucking self, but I let him be a gentleman. He hopped on the driver's side and sped off to wherever he lived.

I must have fallen asleep, because when I woke up he was carrying me to a house that was beautiful. He brought me to his room and went to get a first-aid kit.

"You have a full-length mirror?" I asked, and he walked out the room and came back with two. I set up one in front of me and the other behind me to look at the gash. To say I was outnumbered, the only thing I walked out with was a gash on the back of my head and a few scratches on my face that'd heal with time and cocoa butter. I used the gauze and peroxide to assess it, and it wasn't too bad.

"Did I kill her?" I asked, looking at him through the mirror.

"Fucking right you did, and her friends are dying as we speak. Leave no witnesses," Nyx told me, and I was horrified. Her friends had to die because of her stupid decisions.

"Yo' fucking head gotta be concrete. She hit yo' ass hard as hell." Nyx laughed, and I did too.

"I couldn't feel that shit. She must've hit me with a plastic bottle." I looked at my head and just as I knew, it was a scratch. I bandaged my shit up and stood to move the mirrors, but Nyx beat me to it. I knew I was walking in dangerous territory, but it was what it was.

"You can take a shower. I got a shirt and boxers for you to put on," he told me, and I nodded my head up and down. My body was aching and all I needed was a hot shower.

He showed me where the bathroom was and I ran the water as hot as I could stand it. I peeled my dress off and got in, letting the water soothe my aching bones. It had been a while since I had to beat a bitch that bad. My hands were swollen and bruised because of the force I used to beat her ass. Those were the same hands that helped save people's lives. I should have just stayed my thot ass at home. I felt a cool breeze fly past me and knew Nyx had entered the shower.

Placing his hands on top of mine from behind, he placed them against the tiled wall. His lips touched the back of my neck, and goosebumps were everywhere. His tongue licked and sucked until he reached the arch in my back.

"Damn," I heard him groan as he massaged my ass cheeks in a circle. That shit made me want to turn around, but I didn't.

"Let me have you, please." This nigga was begging and my pussy was leaking. He opened my cheeks and put his entire face in my pussy, and I yelped.

He took his time sucking then licking my clit, and I felt it swell. I moved my hips in a circular motion, riding his tongue. I tried to touch my nipples, but he pushed the top half of my body further into the wall.

"Nah, I got that." His hands snaked the front of my body, palming my breasts. The combination was torture and had my nut sliding down his throat in seconds.

"Oh my gooodddddd." I threw my ass back on his face, suffocating him, and all he did was moan.

After eating his way to my cervix, he stood to his feet and turned me to face him. He opened the condom and slid it on his shaft. I was stuck. I could believe I was about to cheat on Zulu after killing his old bitch. Before I had a chance to regret this moment and walk away, Nyx picked me up and slid me on his dick. We both moaned out as pain for me turned to pleasure as I rode his dick with him standing in place.

I bounced up and down on his dick as I pulled his dreads. I wasn't making love to this nigga, I was fucking him. I made love to my man, and he wasn't it. I nutted on his dick and he put me on my feet. By the time I washed myself, leaving him in the shower and going into the room, I put back on my bloody dress. Guilt had sunken in. I felt like damaged goods. For some reason, I had flashbacks of being raped. I guess that was my guilty conscious, but ain't no sense in crying about it now. I fucked him and now I was ready to go. He walked out the shower and noticed I put my dress back on.

"Bring me back to my car please," I told him without making eye contact. I felt dirty. I needed my girls.

"I got you, let me get my keys," he said and got dressed to bring me to my car. The sun was slowly peaking, I knew I would have to explain myself to my girls when I got there.

13
ZULU

I knew I was fucking up, but Haze got me fucked up. I sent her home for a fucking reason. She was my peace and I wanted it to stay that way. I didn't want her to crossover into this part of my life. She saved lives and I took them bitches and put them in the dirt. When she thought I couldn't see her, I did. I had eyes everywhere, especially on her. When my potnah sent me the video of Haze beating the skin off Taishi, I knew I had to get home and quick. Then the nigga Nyx thought it was cool to touch my lady. This nigga had to know he was about to die.

I ran everything down to Endymion, and he told me to go handle home but don't touch Nyx. Bad as I wanted to off this nigga, my word was bond and I told my brother I wouldn't fuck with him. I took the first flight out and landed, going straight to the house. Imagine my surprise when she wasn't there. I sat on the bed and waited for her because I knew she wasn't still at the fucking club at 6 in the morning. I made myself comfortable and waited to see what fucking lie could she come up with.

I heard the door creak open and her ass stepped in the room. Her dress was intact, but blood covered it. Her hair looked the same and she had a few scratches on her neck, but she was still beautiful. She never saw me on the bed. She threw her purse, keys, and phone on the bed and went straight to the shower. Either she was ignoring me or she just didn't see a nigga. My guess was she didn't see me. Once I heard the shower go on, I gave it a few minutes before I opened the door then the fucking shower curtain. I snatched the door and she jumped, looking at me in horror.

"Where the fuck you been?" I barked at her, and she stood frozen. When she realized it was me, she turned around and started washing her body. I noticed the bandage on the back of her head. She must have had to cut a patch of her hair to put it there. My baby had a bald spot. I stepped in the shower fully clothed and pulled her soapy body into mine. I grabbed the back of her neck.

"Where the fuck you been, Haileaux?" I gripped her neck tighter, but she didn't seem fazed.

"The fuck you mean where I been? I been handling the fucking business that you failed to handle, but don't worry 'bout that, I handled it," she spat at me, and I didn't know whether to be mad at her or turned off. I thought about how Nyx held her securely while shooting in the air to protect her and became livid. I kept a hold of her neck and dragged her out the bathroom naked, sliding all over the floor, and threw her on the bed.

"You fucking with the opp now?" My finger was to her forehead like a gun. She smacked it away.

"The fuck is the opp, nigga?" She stood in my face, not backing down. I pulled out my phone, pulled up the video, and put it in her face.

"Nyx is the fucking opp, so that's what we doing now?" I wanted to choke the life out her short ass.

"Don't be fucking mad at me because a nigga was doing what you should have been doing. Them hoes jumped me, Zulu, but all them bitches in the dirt! You so concerned about what the fuck was going on in California, that you forgetting to take care of home first. Get the fuck away from me, Zulu, before I fuck you up like I fucked yo' bitch up." She pushed past me but didn't get far .

"You fucking that nigga?!" I knew I was fucked when I asked that, because Haze prided herself on loyalty.

"Did you fuck Taishi?" she said, never turning around. "Whatever your answer is, it matches mine." She picked up the lamp and threw it at me. It missed my head by inches. I went behind her and yoked her up and threw her on the bed. I was guilty of fucking Taishi that night in the other book, but she didn't know. I forced her legs open and looked at her neatly waxed pussy. My mouth salivated. I wasn't sure if she fucked that nigga, and I didn't eat behind nobody. Her pussy purred to my dick, and if it wasn't already wet, she fucked that nigga.

"Zulu, get the fuck off of me," she yelled in my face as I fumbled with my belt.

"Fuck no. Since you can't answer my question, I'll find out for myself." I sucked her neck then went down to her breasts. She was trying to fight me, but I could tell she was slowly giving in. I put the tip of my dick to her opening, and she moaned. Her juices coated my shit. The heat from her pussy caused chills to run through my veins. I slid straight inside her and almost nutted. She didn't fuck that nigga, but I still didn't know where she was. Soon as she started to moan and fuck me back, I slid back out and stood to my feet, pulling my jeans up. She sat up, looking at me crazy.

"Nah, I got my answer, and you on punishment. I don't give a fuck where you were. Long as that pussy purrs for me, I'm good. I'm out." I saluted her and I tried to walk out the room. She grabbed me by the back of my shirt, jumping in front of me.

"But you have yet to answer mine. Did you fuck that bitch?" she asked me.

"Does it matter, you killed her, didn't you?" I asked her, and she put her head down. I didn't give a fuck if she felt guilty because I still felt like she fucked that nigga.

"You let that nigga eat my pussy?" I asked her, and she looked me straight in the eye.

"Unlike you, I don't fucking cheat. Yeah, he helped me out because if not, you would have been burying me, motherfucker." She pushed past me to put on her clothes. That shit hit home for me, but I still didn't respect the nigga because of the shit he did with Grela. Nigga still had to die.

"Before you fucking ask, I went to my house to clean my wound and fell asleep. I jumped up and came here because I didn't want Jhenga and Kizzy to worry, but yo' ass was in my bed. It's funny you come running when you see another nigga with my attention. But shit was gravy when you ran in the middle of the night to cater to a bitch that I had to kill out our fucking life." I couldn't argue with that because she was right. I did fuck Taishi and probably would do it again, and the nasty bitch gave me sloppy. It wasn't worth losing Haze's heart.

"I didn't fucking cheat on you," I told her a half-truth.

"But I could bet on my momma that bitch gave you head," she said, and I put my head down in shame.

Whap, whap

Left cheek then right cheek, Haileaux slapped me. I tried to control my temper, but I couldn't.

"Didn't I tell you to keep yo' hands to yo' fucking self , Haze?" I shook her ass like a ragdoll. Rage took over me and I couldn't stop it. She clawed at my hands, but she couldn't overpower me.

"Zulu, you killing her! Let her fucking go." Jhenga jumped on my back, trying to pull my fucking eyeballs out the socket. She beat the top of my head until I let Haze go.

"Go sit in the corner, nigga," Jhenga told me and pointed to the window. She gave me a look, and I knew not to test her because she damn near took a nigga's eye out.

"He needs a fucking time out because he being too reckless," she said out loud and went over to Haze, who was gasping for air with tears falling down her eyes. I looked at her hands as she removed her ring and threw it at me across the room.

"If marrying you gon' be like this, you can fucking keep it." The ring landed in my lap as she left out the room, not looking back.

"What the fuck is wrong with you, Zulu?" Jhenga sat on side of me in the corner. I pulled out my phone and showed her the video.

"Okay, what the fuck that mean?" she asked me. "Looks like he was protecting her. She couldn't fight all six of them bitches by herself." She handed me my phone back and looked at me.

"She didn't come in this bitch until the sun came up. I got a problem with that," I told her, and she laughed.

"Haze is simple. All you had to do was ask her and she would have told you, but knowing your overthinking ass, you probably came in here like the Big Bad Wolf, roughing her up and shit. That's not how Haileaux operates. If she feels like you playing with her, she shuts down. You won't get a word out of her, but she will fight yo' ass. You took shit too far behind your own indiscretions. That shit ain't the look for y'all. Nah me and Nemesis, yeah, I'm 'bout that crazy shit, but Haileaux not." Jhenga stood up after dropping some knowledge. When she got to the door, she turned to face me.

"She was at her fucking house nursing her wounds and fell asleep. She called me when she got there and told me not to worry. But she would be here in the morning, so boom, that's where the fuck she was. See how easy shit could have been." She walked back over to show me her phone, and Haileaux did call her when she left the club.

"Stop overthinking shit when it could be easy. Nah she done took the fucking ring off and threw it at you. You got some serious pussy eating to do to get back in her good graces. I'm going to fix breakfast," she said and disappeared out the door.

14
ENDYMION
CALIFORNIA

This nigga was still in a coma, and I was ready to get back to my wife and family. All this procrastinating was making a nigga wanna take flight and continue what I had going on in New Orleans. I sent Zulu back home because one of his potnahs had a video with Nyx and Haze on it, and this nigga lost it. He went with every intention to kill both of them, but I calmed him down. I told his stupid ass to get the entire story before he started jumping to shit. He was supposed to have eyes on the nigga anyway, so why he got close to the family was mind boggling. I hoped he didn't go fuck shit up with Haze, because she was a good girl.

Nemesis' homesick ass was like a dope feign when it came to Jhenga. We all were losing it, but it was time for action. After I talked to Lady Bug, I showered and got dressed and headed to the hospital. When I walked in the room, Magnolia was sitting up and Zenobia was in the bed with him, kissing his neck. That made me miss Khency even more. I couldn't wait to climb between her thighs and go to sleep.

"Well, excuse me." I cleared my throat and Magnolia looked at me, laughing.

"Excuse me for loving on my damn wife. Nigga, I thought I

was dead." I walked over to dap him up. Zenobia got out the bed and left to give us a minute to speak in private.

"What we 'bout to do about this bitch? I was just waiting on you to wake up," I told him and sat in the chair next to the bed.

"That's already being handled. So I see you met the fam, huh? You ready to take the throne?" he asked me, and I didn't know how to answer that.

"You really don't have much of a choice, nigga. They been keeping eyes on you. They were just waiting on the right time, and the way you and your brothers came through for me, nigga, I owe you my life," he told me, and I felt so guilty for the way I approached the situation with his wife.

"I talked to Meyhani," I told him, and he gave me a hard stare.

"Then you know what it is then." We shook on it and changed the conversation. What's understood didn't need to be explained.

"What the doctors saying?" I asked him.

"Nigga paralyzed from the waist down and Zenobia couldn't handle it. Soon as she told me, she broke down crying, but I told her this wasn't the end of the world. She about to turn our entire basement into a therapy room. The contractors are working on the shit as we speak." Magnolia shook his head. " I should be able to travel this week, but you know we coming to New Orleans to the crowning ceremony," he said, and I looked at him funny.

"Crowning ceremony?" I asked him.

"Yeah, it's about four months from now. The Masons are going to crown you the King of the Mardi Gras Mafia, nigga. That's big shit at home. On some next level type shit. Y'all probably gone move and everything. Big shit." We both laughed, and I couldn't believe I was about to a part of something that I knew almost nothing about. I had to run all this by Khency to see how she felt about it.

"Since I see you straight and Zenobia got shit covered, me

and Nemesis gotta go make sure the home front straight." I raised my hand to salute him.

"Call me if you need me, nigga." We gave each other an unspoken head nod because we knew what was up.

I left my room and curiosity got the best of me because of what Magnolia said, and I went to the floor Grela was being held. I stepped off the elevator and headed to Grela's room. The guards were still in there, and I noticed a nurse in there, I guess checking on her tubes and shit. I slid the door open and stepped inside. As I got closer, I realized it wasn't a nurse but Mahyesha's ass standing next to Grela. She turned to me.

"Shhhhh." I stood there and watched as she cut the wires to the machine that kept Grela alive. Once the cord was cut, Grela grasped for air, and Mahyesha put on a pair of black latex gloves and put her hand over Grela's nose and mouth until her body stopped seizing and went limp. Mahyesha pressed two fingers under her throat to check for a pulse. I'm guessing she didn't find one because she turned to me and started clapping.

"You know I was gon' kill that bitch after you told my son what happened. She was a snake. They were taking too long, so I made the shit happen. I had the guard shut the machines down so they wouldn't alert the desk, and handled my business. She had to go. Any bitch or nigga that poses a threat to my family has to be dealt with. I suggest you handle Nyx before he multiplies." She took off the gloves, threw them against a now dead Grela, and gave me a hug.

"It's time to go home, son, and take care of your family. You have big shoes to fill and everybody needs to be on board. The Masons gon' take care of me and my sons. You focus on your family and we will come together soon. Tell Khency to call me." She hugged me and kissed my cheek before leaving. I thought we were fucked up, but the shit she just pulled was a million-dollar job. The Masons had pull way beyond my control.

15

NEMESIS

"You ready to pop that pussy open for a real nigga?" I told Jhenga on the phone, and she laughed her ass off. I missed that laughed. Fuck, I missed everything about her. Pussy, head, food, I even miss her bad ass attitude. I couldn't wait to wrap my arms around my wife. She made everything better.

"Why you gotta be so stupid? But you know I'mma bust it open, Daddy," she moaned into the phone. "When are y'all coming back? Because Zulu losing his fucking mind," she told me, and I shook my head.

She then broke it down and told me how Zulu damn near killed Haze because she went out and killed Taishi. The only part I didn't like was the fact that now Nyx had something over our heads, so he had to go.

"You need to fix this or he gon' lose Haileaux for good. She left and went home and I had to put his ass on time out." I laughed at that.

"Not time out, bae." I laughed harder.

"Yes, a fucking time out because he was out of line. I had the nigga sitting in the corner facing the wall." I was laughing so hard my stomach hurt.

"After he calmed down, I gave him a pep talk and I think he got the picture." We laughed until I told her I would see her soon.

I thought about calling Zulu but quickly decided against it because he was gon' blame that girl when she did nothing wrong. I got dressed and went downstairs where Endymion was dressed in all black.

"The fuck you 'bout to do? Go to war, nigga?" I asked him because he had a serious look on his face.

"Nah, but I need to holla at you 'bout some shit," he told me as I sat across from him.

"Talk," I told him.

"Magnolia's uncle told me some shit about the Mardi Gras Mafia, and now it's time for us to take over. Instead of King and Queen, we are the three kings. Grela outta here." I looked at him, trying to understand what the fuck that meant.

"Nigga, we about to level up in ways New Orleans ain't never witnessed before. We the fucking plug," he told me. "There's some type of ceremony that's going to be held four months from now at Harrah's in the ballroom where we take the throne," he said, and I rubbed my beard.

"You mean like we call the shots without getting our hands dirty? We don't handle guns, bruh," I told him, because I didn't do the drug empire shit.

"Nah, there's a team for that. We don't touch shit unless we have to. We got an entire empire from drugs to guns to run, you ready for that?" he asked me, and I smiled hard as hell.

"Fucking right I'm ready. I might just upgrade Jhenga and beg her ass to expand out the fucking hood and open up more shops in different states."

"I'm gonna try and get Khency to open her own practice in another state because shit about to change for the better," I told him, and we shook on it. "The only thing now is this nigga Nyx, but I got that covered. We just got to get Zulu in line. Our work here is done. The Masons got Magnolia squared away. It's time for us to head home," Endymion told me, and I was happy as fuck.

I was about to call Jhenga and tell her I was on my way, but it would be a surprise. I wanted to catch her off guard with this good dick.

"Let's go," Magnolia told me, and we hopped in the car and headed to the airport for a five-hour flight.

NEW ORLEANS

It was 5 o'clock when we touched down, and the atmosphere was totally different. We took separate cars because Endymion said he had some shit to handle, and so did I. I went to the crib, showered, and threw on joggers and a t-shirt with some Jordans and hopped in my Charger. I stopped at the jewelry shop and picked up a new engagement ring to replace the old one. This was to new beginnings. I also got Jhenga a heart pendant, a Fendi bag she'd been begging me for, and a dozen pink roses for her. It felt so good to ride the streets of New Orleans without a care in the world. I pulled up by the back door of her shop because I knew she was closed down for the day. On Fridays she closed the shop early because she was always exhausted. I got out my car and snuck through the back door. I searched around for her but didn't see her. I rounded the corner and walked down the hall and paused when I heard her on the phone.

"Bitch, I can't wait for Nemesis to touch down. I'mma suck the skin off his dick and let him fuck me like a dirty dog, bitch. I don't know about you, but I miss my nigga," she said to whoever she was on the phone with, probably Kizzy. She laughed, and I blushed. Hearing her laugh in person was a totally different vibe than hearing that shit on the phone. I couldn't wait to touch every part of her body inside and out. She laughed louder.

"Bitch, you already pregnant, he can't do much else." That had to be Khency because Dymi told me she was pregnant earlier.

"But, bitch," she tried to whisper in the phone, "I'm pregnant too. I haven't told Nemesis yet because I don't know how he gon' feel. That nigga might go ape shit," she whispered, but I heard every word.

"You motherfucking right I'mma go apeshit because you 'bout to have my seed growing in your stomach." She spun around and her face told everything she felt in that moment.

"Bitch, I'mma call you back, my man touched down." She hung the phone up, throwing it on her desk, and jumped up running toward me.

She attacked me, damn near knocking me over and the stuff out my hands. She placed butterfly kisses all over my face and neck. I couldn't hug her back because I had her roses and bags in my hands. I walked in further with her body still wrapped around me and put the stuff on her table. Then I walked over to her desk and sat down in her chair with her still on me. I wrapped my arms around her, and she smelled so fucking good. Flower bomb mixed with whatever shit she used when she did hair. I didn't realize how much I missed that smell until I smelled it. My hands grabbed her face and pulled her down to kiss me as she fumbled with my belt. She had on a dress for easy access. She pulled my dick out and lifted up and mounted my shit.

"You gon' have my baby?" My voice was strained because her pussy was gripping my dick, sucking the life out of it.

"Yes, baby," she moaned as she twirled her hips against me.

"You gon' be my wife?" I asked her as she got up and turned around with her back against my chest. She stood and bent over, giving me a full view of her pink pussy. She sat down and went crazy on my shit. She was bouncing so fast my dick felt like it was about to detach from my body. Her juices wet me up, and I scooted toward the end of the chair because she was trying to fuck me out of it.

"Damn, slow down." I tried to grip her hips to slow her pace, but she moved my hands.

"Bae, I been waiting on this dick. Let me have my way," she moaned, and I grabbed the back of her neck to dive deeper. I wanted to feel every crevice of her pussy because I needed it to keep me sane. After we both nutted, she got up off my now soft dick and went into her bathroom. She cleaned herself and brought a warm cloth to clean me and threw the towel in the garbage can by her desk.

"What you got me, Nemesis?" she said when she finally noticed the bags on the table.

"Wait, let me give you this first." I went in my pocket and pulled out the box that held her new ring. I opened the box and her eyes lit up.

"I have a ring already, babes," she told me while looking at her finger.

"But this is a new beginning for us. We got some shit to discuss." I took her old ring off and slid the new one on.

"I think I like this one better anyway." She smiled as I kissed her lips. We locked up the shop and headed to our home to fuck and discuss our future plans.

16
ENDYMION

I had been watching this nigga's every move for the past three hours. As bad as I wanted to go home to Lady Bug, this had to be done. I was sitting right outside Basin Street Lounge waiting on this nigga Nyx to come out. He'd went in with some jump off bitch with too small clothes on that barely covered her ass.

"Man, where this nigga at?" I looked at my phone and it was getting late. I was ready to move on this nigga, but he was taking too long. I had to get him though. I wasn't about to give this nigga time to create an army against us.

Not only was this shit about KOE, but this was personal too. I knew Haze fucked that nigga, but I would never tell Zulu. That would kill him. I would confront Haze with it because that was some down bad shit she was doing or did. When you think a motherfucker wasn't watching you, they were. I saw the shit past the fucking video. He took her to his home and they fucked. She felt guilty and left just the way she'd went in. I had hittas all over watching my family. Jhenga made up the perfect lie for her, but that's another story that would never get told, because I understood. I lied for my brothers so many times that I couldn't blame Jhenga for lying for her girl. Fuck, I was keeping this shit from my brother, but it was what it was. I kept the location on all their phones because of the shit that Grela had pulled. What they didn't know was the shit was still turned on. When Haze called Jhenga, she was in that nigga's house, because I tracked her history. Maybe Jhenga didn't know that Haze was really by that nigga, but I knew she killed Taishi and that Nyx was bragging about the shit in the hood. Talking like he got a real hitta on his team and it's a female.

I hated a nigga than ran his mouth about everything like a bitch. Real niggas moved in silence, but he was never silent from the beginning. He thought Grela was gonna help him, but clearly that's a dead case. I started playing Candy Crush on my phone when the nigga walked out the club with the same bitch he walked in with. They got in the car and pulled off with me not too far behind them. I noticed them going to his place. This nigga lived in a gated community, but there was always a way around anything. Once he parked and got out the car, groping and kissing all on his bitch, I sat there and screwed my silencer on my gun and got out the car. I raised my hood over my head and jumped the fence to get in his house. I waited a minute because I knew he was about to fuck, and I wanted to catch them in the act. The nigga had to be sloppy drunk because he left the fucking door open, so I walked right in. I walked around the house taking in the scenery. Nigga had a nice home, but it was about to be someone else's home in a minute. I heard moans coming from upstairs and headed up the spiral staircase until I got to the top. I heard louder moans to my left and went with my move and kicked the door off the hinges.

"You 'bout to die in that pussy, nigga," I told him as he jumped up and pushed the bitch off him. He tried to go for his gun and I shot his right hand. "Na, nigga, you really got caught with yo' hands in the cookie jar." I laughed, shaking my head, taunting him. Whoever this bitch was kept screaming until she ran out of sound because I shot one to her dome, sending her flying against the headboard.

"Get yo' bitch ass up," I told him, and he got up and sat in the chair. I walked up to him and looked in his eyes.

"You thought it was okay to fuck my brother's wife?" I cocked my head to the side, waiting for his answer.

"She wanted me," he yelped out in pain. I ain't give a fuck if she wanted him or not.

"So, if I call her right now, she gon' tell me she wanted to fuck you and betray my brother?" I put the tip of my gun to his right knee.

"Nah man, it wasn't like that. I had to get my hittas to help her because she killed ole girl." He trembled, scared for his life, as he should be. "She's kin to the mayor, I couldn't leave her hanging." He tried to save face, but his life was already over.

"You think I give a fuck if she's related to the fucking mayor? That nigga fuck with me now," I told him and shot his kneecap out. He yelped in pain, and I stuffed his boxers in his mouth because he was screaming like a bitch.

"Don't cry now, nigga. Were you crying when you were knee deep in my sis-in-law's pussy?" I asked him, but he didn't answer.

"You also thought Grela was gon' save yo' ass when y'all switched positions for the drop that ended in my nigga getting shot." My gun was to his head, damn near taking it off.

"He can't walk, so you won't either," I told him and shot his other kneecap out.

"Ok, ok, ok. I thought Grela was gon' let me in y'all camp, but I see that isn't happening. That's the only reason why I agreed, man." He tried to talk but couldn't.

"Well, now you about to be where Grela is," I said and riddled his body with bullets. I pulled out my burner phone and called the crew. "Clean up on aisle nine, pronto." I disconnected the call and went home to my family.

As I rode the dark streets of my city, I knew I couldn't tell Zulu that Haze fucked that nigga. That would be some shit I would keep to myself because he'd just found his happy place and

I wasn't about to fuck that up. Speaking of that nigga, he was ringing my line.

"What's up, nigga? I hear you in the doghouse." I laughed at his stupid ass.

"That nigga Nemesis and Jhenga talk too fucking much. Yeah, but I ain't fucked up with it. She left a nigga and I'm cool with that." I knew it was a lie because he called me. He only called me when he wanted me to step in and make shit right.

"Where you at, nigga?" he asked me out of the blue.

"Just came from handling some business. Why, what's up?" I asked him, already knowing the answer.

"I need you to fix this shit, man, because she ain't even taking my calls. I think she blocked me." He laughed.

"After the story that was told to me, nigga, you lucky she didn't flash out on yo' ass and fuck you up like she did ole girl." We laughed but shit was serious.

"I got you, just give a nigga a few days," I told him and hung up the phone.

I pulled into my driveway and my heart fluttered. I couldn't wait to see Khency and my son. The peace I felt when I was with her made me feel like I could conquer the world. I hopped out the car and headed to the house. I used my key and opened the door to pitch blackness. I knew she was probably sleep, so I decided to take a shower downstairs then go upstairs and cater to my wife. My dick got hard just thinking about how warm and juicy her pussy felt.

I took the steps two at a time and noticed the door was closed but the light was still on. I creaked the door open and to my surprise, Lady Bug was sitting in the middle of our bed with only lace panties on, breastfeeding Potato. The sight almost brought tears to my eyes. I could only imagine when her lil' pudge got big and started poking out. I could tell she wanted to get up and jump in my arms, but his mouth had a vice grip on her right breast while his hand cradled the other. Her leg was trembling she was so excited to see a nigga. It was like seeing me like a celebrity or some shit. She tried not to move so much because he was falling asleep.

"I can wait," I told her, and her leg stop trembling. Her smile was wide as fuck and made a nigga blush. Her face was already flushed, so I could only imagine what my face looked like.

I slowly sat on the bed and watched in awe as she fed him until she was sure he was knocked out. I watched on as she slowly got up to put him in his bed. Her voluptuous ass ate her panties, and my dick rose for the occasion. She was holding him, so she couldn't pull them out her ass as she bent over to put him down. When she stood back up, she pulled her panties out her ass and turned to me. I stood up to receive her and she ran to me, breasts flopping all over, but that shit was sexy as fuck. She jumped in my arms, wrapping her legs around me, making both of us fall to the bed. She rained kisses all over my neck, and I moaned in response. Her tongue glided from the base of my neck to my lips. It's something about the way she did that shit that made a nigga's knees weak.

"I missed you so fucking much," she whispered in my ear as I grabbed her waist. I ran my hands up and down her spine, watching her shiver from my touch. I could stay in this position with her forever. Her fucking skin was a work of art and it was all mine. I sat up with my back against the headboard with her still on my lap and kissed her softly. She reached under her, inside my boxers, pulling my dick out. She lifted up and pulled her panties to the side to sit on it. We both moaned in satisfaction. She rolled her ass a little bit to adjust to my girth because it had been a while, and I was a second from busting.

"Fuck." I pressed deeper into her to make sure I was all the way in. I gripped her hips tight as fuck to stop her slightest movement.

"You ready to talk now?" she asked me as my head fell against the headboard. I didn't wanna talk, but I knew she needed this conversation.

"Is she gone?" she asked in a child-like voice, and I nodded my head up and down.

"Did you do it?" she asked like she was afraid of the answer.

"No," I told her honestly, because I didn't.

"Okay." She shrugged her shoulder and bent down to kiss me.

"Why do I feel like you have more to tell me?" she asked, looking into my eyes, and I fucking melted.

"I do, but right now all I want you to do is ride this dick like the stallion you are," I moaned as she moved her hips in a circle, never breaking eye contact. Her arms circled my neck as I pinched her nipples. She grinded deeper, sending me on a high that weed could never give me.

"Ummmm, Poppa," she moaned in my ear as she rode me nice and slow. I bit her neck to stifle my moans to not wake up the baby. I needed this. She was my safe haven. Nothing mattered when I was knee deep inside my wife's pussy. I could block out the world and the people in it just for the taste of her skin. She rocked back and forth, rubbing her clit against my shaft with every movement. I gave her control of our orgasm because she deserved it and so much more. Little did she know, she had complete control over my heart.

I woke up the next morning feeling like a million bucks. I rolled over to a sleeping Khency. I just watched as she lay on her back. The bottom half of her body was covered, but her areolas were looking straight at me. My mouth watered. I had to taste her. I hadn't tasted her in weeks, and a nigga was hungry and only she could cure my appetite. Her chest rose and fell and I could tell she was tired from all the positions I bent her thick ass in last night. I reached over and pinched at one of her breasts, and she didn't move. I reached over and sucked one and slid my hand under the cover to massage her swollen clit. She was wet as fuck. I slid my middle finger inside her and she stirred a little. I moved under the cover and came face to face with her pussy. I opened her lips up and sucked her clit, applying pressure.

"Oh my god, Poppa." She threw her pussy in my face and I ate that shit up.

"Be quiet and let yo' nigga eat." I hummed in her pussy as I put two fingers inside of her. Her entire body lifted off the bed as I sucked her clit and fingered her insides.

"Move, bae, I gotta pee," she yelled, and I hoped she didn't wake Potato up.

"Nah, that ain't piss, bae, just let that shit rip," I told her, feeling her wall grip my fingers.

"Fuuucckkkkk," she yelled as she squirted all over my face and beard, and I licked that shit up until she was dry. I came up for air and kissed her lips so she could taste what I tasted.

"That shit was so good I might buy you a short set," she told me, and we both laughed and made sweet love until Potato hated on a nigga and started crying.

17

JHENGA

"What the fuck Endymion wanna meet me and Khency for?" I shook Nemesis awake as I looked at the text message on my phone. It was 8 in the morning and this nigga summoned me to his house.

"I don't fucking know. The nigga sent you the message not me," Nemesis growled and turned over and went back to sleep.

"But he yo' fucking brother. Maybe he text me by accident." I mushed his ass, but he didn't move. We had been eating, fucking, and sleeping for the past two weeks with no interruptions, and here this nigga go.

"If I gotta go, then you coming too." I pushed Nemesis hard as fuck, and that got a reaction out his ass.

"Push me again and I'mma knock you the fuck out. Stop playing before I knock them fucking eyelashes off yo' face." He rolled over on his back, and I could see his morning wood through the covers. I knew just how to wake his ass up. He was never too tired for morning head.

Endymion better have something damn near death to tell us. It was too early in the morning to get out my warm bed to see what he wanted. It better be something dealing with Kizzy, because this nigga started calling since I didn't answer my text messages. Why the fuck he didn't call Nemesis with this bullshit?

I peeked my head under the cover and placed my hand around his dick. I stroked him up and down until he was hard as fuck. I licked the tip as pre-cum tickled the tip of my tongue before I swallowed him whole. This nigga still didn't move. My hand massaged his balls, and he stretched his body out.

"What the fuck?" I felt him pull the cover up, and my eyes met his as my head bobbled up and down.

"Damn, bae, that's how you feeling?" he moaned, bringing his hand to the back of his head, guiding my rhythm. I let him have that because I wanted his ass to get up. He knew I hated when he held the back of my head, but I was on a mission. He pulled the cover all the way off. He pulled my hair back so he could fuck my mouth just the way he wanted to. I came up, connecting my saliva with his pre-cum and making it sloppy for him. Slob built up in my mouth and I spat on his dick, and I felt his ass cheeks tighten.

"Yo' nasty ass," he moaned as his nut erupted in my mouth and I drank it all.

"Nah get yo' ass up so we can go see what Dymi want." I smacked his thigh and got up to take care of my hygiene.

After I got out the shower, I realized Nemesis was still in the fucking bed sleep. I walked to the foot of the bed and ran the tips of my nails across the bottom of his feet. He hated that shit. He jumped like I stuck my finger in his ass.

"Motherfucker, didn't I tell you to leave me alone." He was up on his feet and in my face in seconds.

"And didn't I tell you yo' fucking brother keep texting and calling me to come to his house? Nah get dressed so we can go, nigga," I told him, not backing down. He should have known that I could repeat anything I said twice because I was that bitch. My mouth was real disrespectful, and I was only submissive when I was getting dicked down. He walked away from me ass naked and got in the shower. I didn't give a fuck how mad he was. If I was going, then so was he.

When we walked into the house and into the living room, I noticed Khency sitting with Khenzington on her lap near Endymion. Zulu sat on the opposite side of them with his head in his hands. He looked stressed. Hair in a messy bun. Looking like he ain't ate in weeks. Hails really had that nigga fucked up.

I tugged at Nemesis' arm discreetly, being messy so he could look at Zulu.

"Damn, nigga, what fucking bus ran you over?" He laughed and looked at Zulu, but Zulu didn't. He reached behind his back and sat his gun on the table. Nemesis pulled his and sat it on the table as well.

"Nigga, Haze really got yo' mind fucked up to pull a gun on me. You pulling it but are you gon' use it?" I saw the scowl on Nemesis' face.

"This ain't checkers, nigga," Zulu told him, and I was confused. What the fuck checkers had to do with them about to shoot each other?

"Fuck checkers, nigga, this chess," Nemesis said, picking up his gun. "I don't miss, nigga, but you know that already," Nemesis said.

"And I'mma sniper, nigga, so you know how I'm coming." I looked at Endymion with pleading eyes because both these niggas were trippin'. Khency just sat there and covered her baby's eyes, not saying a word.

"Nigga just mad because Haze left his dumb ass." That's all it took for Zulu to leap across the room and attack Nemesis. They rained blows on each other until Potato started crying and Dymi broke it up.

"Y'all too fucking old for this shit. Nemesis, learn how to keep yo' fucking mouth closed, and Zulu, nigga, you need to get it together, bruh, because shit about to change," Endymion barked at them.

"Man, fuck that nigga," Zulu spat at Nemesis while tucking in his busted lip.

"I love you too, Princess." Nemesis looked at Zulu and they both laughed like they weren't just killing each other moments ago. They grabbed their guns and put them back and got down to the real reason we were all here. I can't lie, though, shit felt different without Hails around.

"This Mardi Gras Mafia shit is real. We will be crowned the three kings a few months from now, so I need everyone in place. Everything will be handed over to us and then broken down to fit everyone's needs. Changes will be made. The Masons will partner up with us and break shit down," Endymion told them. "We have teams of heavy hittas working under us that will do the foot work. All we do is give commands," he told them.

"How the fuck all this came about?" Zulu asked.

"Grela was trying to become queen, but her snake ass was trying to persuade us into working with her when it was our empire from the beginning," Endymion said, looking at his brothers. My mouth dropped open.

"So where is Grela now?" I had to put my two cents in.

"In memory lane," Endymion said. My eyes darted to Kizzy, but she kept her head down. I was guessing she knew what happened because her face was void of emotion.

"Outside of that, I need y'all help to get Haze to forgive my brother. He may be a little fucked up, but the love he has for Haze should never be doubted," Endymion said, looking at me and Kizzy.

"You didn't see what the fuck I saw. He was trying to kill her," I told Endymion.

"I wasn't here, but I saw it. I have cameras all over this motherfucker. Zulu was wrong and now he's trying to get right." Endymion looked at me like I had the answers.

"Man, this what the fuck you called us over here for early in the morning?" Nemesis was still angry about that shit.

"Boy, shut up, we here now," I told him and stuck my tongue out at him.

"I'mma cut that motherfucker off, keep playing." He kissed me and I laughed.

"So how you trying to win my friend back, nigga?" I looked at Zulu and I knew he was going through it. He shrugged, and I felt sorry for him. I knew Hails still wanted to be with him because she told me when I talked to her, but he didn't need to know that. She was afraid of him though. She told me he'd never lost his temper like that, but I told her he was just jealous because another nigga saved her when he should have. It was ego shit. Looking at him now looking all stupid and sad, I knew it was an ego trip.

"Marry her." I got up and sat next to him and put my short ass arm around his shoulder.

"I can't, she threw the ring at me," he said.

"Okay, go buy her another one, duh," I told him, and that got a smile out of him.

"Ohhh, and her birthday is next week. Surprise her with a wedding. We'll get her dressed in true hood fashion like we going out, but y'all will be at the VFW hall waiting our arrival with the minister and the rest of the crew. Hails is very quiet and private so trust me, she'll love it. Now we can get her there for you, but we can't get her to marry you. You gon' have to beg like Jodeci, nigga," I told him and got up.

"Is there anything else, Dymi? Because yo' brother gon' fucking die if he don't go back to sleep." Dymi nodded his head, and I grabbed Nemesis by the front of his shirt and dragged him out the door.

18

HAILEAUX

Work. Eat. Sleep. Repeat was my routine since I left Zulu. I missed him so fucking much that the shit he left at my house I had it in the bed with me just so I could smell him. He had me scared of him though. I really thought he was going to kill me that night in his brother's house. I didn't give a fuck if he was fucking Taishi, I killed that insecurity. He couldn't fuck her anymore, but I did feel bad for fucking Nyx. But fuck, the nigga was sexy. The way he came through for me was a fucking turn on. I didn't fuck Nyx out of spite. I did it because I wanted to. He didn't force me. I rode that dick like Meg and wasn't apologizing for it.

I had been doing doubles for the past two weeks when I realized my birthday was three days away. I told my boss that I wanted three weeks off and she obliged because I had been doing favors when she needed me. It was the end of my shift. I walked to my car, hopped in, and connected my phone to the radio. I needed the sounds of India Arie to mend my broken heart. Before I could play a song, my phone rang. It was 5 in the fucking morning. Even the hens hadn't started cackling yet. My heart skipped a beat as Zubae showed up on my phone. I didn't want to answer it because I knew if I did, I would fall back into his trap and all would be forgiven. I picked up my phone and hit ignore and made my way home.

Once I got home, showered, and put my bonnet on, I was out like a light. I didn't even eat. I hadn't eaten much anyway because I missed Zulu feeding me. He transformed into a monster right before my eyes, and that didn't sit right with me. I was still in love with him, but he traumatized the fuck out of me when he choked me. I saw that shit every time I closed my eyes unless I took the medication that my doctor gave me. Y'all thought it was a game, but it wasn't. I'm quiet for a reason because once I turn up, there was no turning down. It killed me to ignore his calls, but I had to, to maintain my peace.

After sleeping the day away, the sun came and went twice, my ringing phone brought me out my slumber. It was Jhenga calling, and I ignored her ass too. She was another one begging me to forgive Zulu. I would, but when I felt like it. His ass needed to be taught a lesson, and I was the teacher. When I didn't answer the phone, my doorbell rang. How the fuck did they get past security? I'mma report their ass. Then I heard keys in the keyhole, so I knew that was Khency or Jhenga, maybe both. These bitches just didn't understand that I didn't wanna be bothered. I wanted to wallow in my misery until I felt like getting up. I heard the door open and threw the cover over my head.

"Oh no, bitch, get up. It's yo' birthday and we celebrating." That was Jhenga's loud mouth ass, and I knew Khency wasn't too far behind.

"Oh no, bitch, get up and wash yo' ass. That nigga ain't depressed like this, but he do look bad though," Khency said, and I got a little happy. At least he was hurting too. Jhenga snatched the cover off my body and held her nose.

"Bitch, you stannnkkkk! Get the fuck up and take a shower and meet us in the kitchen." They opened the curtains, letting the sun burn my eyes.

I dragged myself to the shower and realized it was my

fucking birthday! I was working so much that I didn't even realize that it was my born day. I needed my hair done, nails, and my ass and pussy waxed, because I knew these two heffas had some shit planned for today.

After taking care of my hygiene, I put on a pair of skinny jeans, a red fitted tee, and a pair of Jordans. I let my hair remain in its natural state because I knew Jhenga would do my hair later. I met them in the kitchen and when they saw me, they both screamed.

"My bitch bad, badder than yours." We hugged three ways. That was our thing we did when we were about to get into some shit.

"I know y'all got the day planned for me, so what's the first stop?" I asked as they ate Golden Grahams, sitting on top the counter. I swear some things never changed.

"First we going to get you something to wear at the Mall of Louisiana, and while we there we can do nails. Then we going to European Waxed and letting them take care of that ass and kitty. We gon' come back here, smoke us a blunt, get dressed, and go wherever the wind takes us." They ran the entire day down to me, and I smiled. They didn't give a fuck what depression I was in, I knew my girls would be there to make my day special.

"Well, when y'all hoes finish eating my cereal, I'll be ready go to," I told them and went to take my trash out.

Something as simple as taking the trash out made me think about that nigga. Zulu was embedded in my soul. I went to sleep and woke up thinking about this nigga. I just couldn't shake the look in his eyes when he choked me. Hate, rage, and larceny lived within him for me, and that shit hurt like hell. I wasn't even that mad when I found out he was still fucking with Taishi. I killed her. Her death didn't happen like that in my head, but I caught the bitch slipping and all common sense left out the window. If I didn't kill her when I did, she wouldn't have stopped until Zulu killed her. Shit would have been gruesome.

"God, I miss him," I whispered to myself and looked toward

the beautiful sky above. I needed a sign, just any sign that Zulu and I were meant to be and I'd take it. I threw my trash away and walked back in the house just as Khency and Jhenga were coming out. Khency had my purse and Jhenga had my phone. She locked the door and turned to me.

"Bitch, Zulu called you 15 times in 10 fucking minutes." I laughed because he had been doing that for the past two weeks.

"I know, but I ain't ready for all that yet. That nigga tried to kill me," I told them as we walked to the car.

"Bitch, me and Nemesis try to kill each other every other fucking day and we still together, so make it make sense, sis," Jhenga told me, and Khency laughed.

"Bitch, I had to go upside Endymion's head before behind some stupid shit he did, soooo what you saying?" Khency rolled her eyes and I chuckled.

"Y'all didn't see the death in his eyes when he was choking me. That shit gave me nightmares. Bitches, I take medicine for the nightmares just to sleep at night. Can we say Xanax for 500, Alex?" That left their mouths open. I'd tried to smoke a blunt at night, but that shit made me more paranoid. Wine didn't do it, so I went to my doctor.

"Yeah, that's what I thought. Y'all bitches used to fighting them niggas, but y'all know when provoked, I go too far and cause too much damage." I walked away from them and got into Khency's G-wagon.

We went to the mall and balled the fuck out. I even got myself an iPhone 13. I had to upgrade myself as a birthday present to myself. I also bought me another Apple watch and Airpods to complement my phone. After that, these bitches wanted to go to a boutique to get some Givenchy dress that Jhenga thought I would look cute in. It was a soft pink, fitted dress that left little to the imagination. It was a floor-length silk dress with a long split up the leg. Shit looked sexy as hell on me. I didn't know where the fuck I was going to wear it to, but I wanted it. That was Khency's birthday gift to me, and next we went to Saks per Jhenga's ass. She bought me the floral pink, spike Gucci tennis with the matching bag to go with my dress. These bitches definitely had something up their sleeves, because they didn't get shit for themselves. I made sure to get my nails light pink because Khency said I was wearing the dress and shit tonight when we went out.

After we left the mall, we stopped at Ruth's Chris to eat because Jhenga said I'd need to eat before we took shots. I ordered me a pineapple cocktail with a shot of Everclear. I was turning 24, so it was about to be on and popping. We smoked a blunt on the way back to the house even though these bitches were pregnant. They had virgin drinks and would be for the rest of the night.

While Jhenga did my hair, Khency got dressed and did her makeup. Jhenga washed my hair in the sink, blow dried it, and straightened it, and it hung almost to my waist. She even cut me some Chinese bangs, giving me a sassy look. She even put highlights in the bangs to give me an edge and sex appeal. I took a quick shower and slid on my pink lace thong. My dress didn't require a bra, thank God, because I hated wearing them. Khency put my tennis shoes on like I was her fucking child. I laughed at the thought. They always treated me like a baby and sometimes it was annoying. I stood in front of the floor-length mirror and took my body in. My silhouette was of a short Coke bottle, and I felt sexy as hell.

"My bitch do shit that yo' bitch wish she could." Jhenga came behind me and gave me my gold hoop earrings.

"Okay, big ole steppa," Khency said as all three of us stood in front of the mirror. I noticed these bitches had on dresses similar to mine but different shoes. The dresses and sneakers shit was the thing now, but I felt we were overdressed and I didn't even know where we were going.

"Where the fuck we going dressed like we going to the prom?" I asked them as we inspected our dresses.

"Kevin Gates got a concert in Dreams and we going," Khency said, smiling.

"It's yo' birthday, bitch, we going wherever the wind takes us," Jhenga said as she grabbed the pink lipstick and applied it to my lips.

We grabbed our phones and purses and headed out the door for a night of fun.

After taking another exit, I realized that Jhenga was going in a different direction from the club.

"You going the wrong way, bitch," I told her, and she looked at me and rolled her eyes.

"I gotta stop at the Hilton Riverside to see why the fuck Nemesis keep blowing my phone up," she said, keeping her eyes on the road.

"Why he at the Hilton?" I asked out of curiosity.

"He said the Masons were in town because they found Nyx's head floating in the river." I almost threw up in my mouth.

"Yeah, I know you fucked that nigga, but looks like somebody got to him before Zulu could. Nah be easy and enjoy your night." She continued to weave in and out of traffic, heading to the hotel.

19
ZULU

I didn't know how Jhenga pulled this shit off, but she did. Nemesis rented out the entire top floor of the Hilton Riverside Hotel. Jhenga hired a planner to decorate the room with pink balloons and glass sculptures everywhere. They had bitches dressed like angels hanging from the ceiling playing the violin.

All the tables and chairs were decorated with pink table cloths with gold trimming. Simple but beautiful. I hoped like fuck Jhenga knew what she was doing and that Haze forgave a nigga, because I couldn't see my life without her. Me and my brothers were dressed in Givenchy jeans and Gucci sneakers. I had on a matching black button down with my hair and goatee lined to perfection. I had to show out for my baby. I even got us new rings in hopes that she would forgive a nigga.

The caterers had prepared all Haze's favorite foods, seafood fettuccini with cheese biscuits, fried chicken and fish, and broccoli cheese balls with bacon. She was a simple woman and I loved that about her. It didn't take much to please her. I had Nemesis put down a white chaser to greet her at the door when they did come in. I was nervous as fuck because I didn't know what the outcome of this shit would be. Listening to Jhenga, I shouldn't have done this shit and just kept begging her. Eventually, she'd take me back.

"Nigga, hit the blunt and calm down before the pastor get here." Endymion handed me the blunt and I toked it straight to the head. I needed something to calm my nerves because the suspense was killing me.

"What if she don't show up, nigga?" Nemesis walked up, laughing his ass off. "Jhenga did say Haze was looking fucked up when I talk to her earlier," he finished, taking the blunt from me.

"Nigga, after all the money we spent on this shit, she better show up or I'mma drag her ass in here," Endymion said, and I laughed at that. I cleared my throat and tried to fan the smoke away as the pastor walked into the room and to us.

"You ready, son?" he asked me.

"Yes, but the question is, will she say yes?" I told him, and he winked his eye.

"Well, looks like we about to find out. Khency just text me saying they were on their way up," Endymion said as I got into position. The double doors opened, and Haze fell in, not paying attention as Tink started to sing.

I done fell in love with the real thing
Even though you make me mad I could never leave
When I met you I was hoping it would last
And it ain't about your money or your bag
My feelings on the line
And you got me making time
I ain't never met a man who could love me like you
You put me on the top
And I like the way we rock
And I promise I'ma love you till my heartbeat stops
More than a friend
You my one and only
You tell me it's real
And I feel it when you hold me

Love me, touch me, and tell me that you need it
You my dog and I'm with you for a reason
Keep it real if it's anything you need
I be jumpin' in my car
Give no fuck about the speed
I'ma do what all I can just to show you that I got ya
Sing to you like an opera babe

Tink sang as the music played in the background, and Haze looked up at me. That was her favorite song. I didn't think she realized what was happening because she tried to push against Jhenga and Khency to get back out the door, but they pushed back until she was on the white trail.

"Start walking, bitch," Jhenga thought she whispered as they stood on each side of her and started walking down the makeshift aisle.

Haze's eyes misted and held mine the entire time they walked. She was about to cry, and I wanted to run to her and hold her the rest of the way. I didn't know if they were happy tears or if she was mad because her friends had tricked her, but I hoped like hell she wanted me. She started walking slow on purpose. I thought she was about to turn and run until Jhenga grabbed her arm. She got halfway to me and I couldn't wait anymore. I walked away from my brother and met her halfway. Jhenga and Khency backed away, leaving us alone in the middle of the floor. When I got in front of her, I towered over her, looking into her eyes.

"You know I don't like attention, Zulu." She cut her eyes at me.

"Look at me. It's just us. Nobody but me and you," I whispered to her, and I saw the tears falling down her cheeks. I wiped them away with my thumb, and she flinched. That broke me.

"You know I would never do anything to hurt you, right? I lost my cool at the thought of another man in yo' face, but to actually see that shit…" I paused because I felt my anger coming. "That shit fucked with my soul that I wasn't there when you needed me. I don't want you to ever fear me, Haze. We built our foundation on love because that's what we have, right?" I asked her, and she put her head down. I lifted her chin with my finger.

"I'm up here. Tell me you don't love me and we can pretend this shit never happened and walk away single," I told her, and she cried.

"I thought you were going to kill me, Zulu." Her face turned a shade of red.

"I wasn't going to kill you. I let my anger get the best of me, and I declare and decree right here that it will never happen again," I told her, grabbing her hands and kissing her fingertips. She looked at me, still debating, biting her bottom lip.

I got down on both of my knees and hugged her waist tight as fuck. She ran her hands through my man bun, and I hugged her tighter.

"I love you more than I love myself. It pained me more than you know for me to grip yo' neck like that. It kills a part of me every time I think about that night. I can't breathe without you, Haze. I'm suffocating out here without you. Please, marry me," I begged lowly so only she could hear me.

"Nah, we ain't doing shit quietly, nigga, go live," she told me and pulled out her cellphone and went to her Instagram app and clicked the live button. "Let the entire world know that we getting married today." I rose to my feet and took her phone and put my face in the camera.

"Today I am marrying the love of my life. On her birthday we will declare our love for one another for the world to see."

I picked her up and threw her over my shoulder and walked the rest of the way to the pastor. I handed the phone to Nemesis so he could video everything. I looked, and Jhenga and Khency had their phones out going live too.

"Bitch, everybody watching this shit," Jhenga said as I put Haze on her feet. I pulled out our rings and gave her mine.

After we repeated our vows after the pastor, we put our rings on and I kissed her before he could pronounce us man and wife. I missed this woman with my entire heart, and I couldn't wait to show her just how much for the rest of our lives. I hugged and kissed her face, neck, and chest as they recorded everything. I didn't give a fuck what they did. Today was the best day of my life.

After the ceremony and everybody had went to their suites, it was just me and Haze in the room with the DJ.

"I love you so much," I whispered in her ear as we swayed to the music that was playing.

"I love you too," she whispered to me as I kissed her lips. Everything about this moment was perfect. I couldn't wait to get back to our suite and have married make-up sex with my wife. My life couldn't get any better than this.

20

ENDYMION

4 MONTHS LATER

"Poppa, I can't fit this dress. I'm too fat to be trying to look sexy, fuck them people," Lady Bug said as she stood in the mirror with me behind her trying to zip her dress. It was the night that me and my brothers would be crowned kings, and the Alexander McQueen maternity dress I'd gotten her made every curve, including her baby bump, show.

"It's not too tight." I finished the zipper and shrugged. "You look sexy as fuck to me." I kissed her bare shoulder as she slipped her feet into her McQueen sequin flats.

"This shit too small, unzip it," she said, out of breath.

"Fuck no, this the third dress you tried on, and I want you in this one so you can match my fly," I told her, and she frowned.

"You got Khenzington ready?" she asked me, and on cue, he ran his bad ass in our room full force into her belly.

My life was the shit. I would have never thought that I would have a family and be a married man. I was never a nigga that ran through hoes, but I never thought I would be married with kids

"Slow down, nigga, ya brother in there." I pulled him back.

"You gon' put his hair in a ponytail?" I hated that she let his hair grow out and it hung past his ass. I watched as she sat on the bed and he eased his way to her.

"Give me a rubber band." She rolled her eyes and fingered his hair into a bun. On many occasions I told her to cut his hair because he was not a fucking female, but the most he got was a line-up.

I leaned on the wall and watched as he twisted and turned because he hated for anyone to touch his hair. My lil' nigga matched my fly. He had on his Gucci loafers with his skinny pants and shirt with his vest that matched his mother's dress.

"There, all done since Daddy wanted your hair in a ponytail." I laughed.

She stood up with him in front of her and I got behind her. My hand rubbed her belly as my son kicked her ass. Everywhere I touched, he kicked.

"He always do that shit when you touch my stomach." We laughed as Potato ran out the room. I grabbed her hand and made her sit on the bed. My hand ran up her thighs until they got to her naked ass.

"Where the fuck is your panties, Lady Bug?" I asked as I kissed her inner thighs.

"It's too hot and you know my thighs rub," she moaned out, letting her head fall back.

"Potato gon' come back," she said with her hands guiding my head right where she wanted it.

"This ain't gon' take long." I pushed her legs apart and slurped on her clit. I had her coming in seconds. Just as I wiped my mouth, he came running in the room.

"Told ya." I winked my eyes up as I pulled her from the bed so I could clean the mess I made.

I put her bracelet on along with the iced-out Cartier she had been asking me for to complement my Rolex. Simple diamond earrings were in her ear, and Jhenga hooked her up with some type of updo that displayed her beautiful features. We'd discussed her opening her private firm in another state because I was over New Orleans. It was time for a fresh start. She said she wanted to deliver the baby here and then we could leave, and I agreed. We both held lil' man's hand as we went down the stairs to her G-wagon. I made sure they were safe inside before I went to lock the house up, and we made our way to Harrah's New Orleans' ballroom.

21
NEMESIS

"Hurry yo' wide ass up or we gon' be late, Jhenga, damn," I yelled in the bedroom while she showered. It was true though. Jhenga was almost five months pregnant and she was wide as all outside. She looked like she was carrying twins, but the doctor said it was only one baby. Her hips had spread wide and I loved hitting that ass from the back when she wasn't being stingy with the pussy. She swore I was gonna hit the top of my baby's head with the tip of my dick. I even asked her doctor and she said it was perfectly fine for us to fuck, but Jhenga wasn't feeling that shit.

Earlier, when I walked in the room to her butt ass naked with her legs wide open, I knew it was gonna be a good day. I put the pound game on her ass and ate her pussy to make her feel better. Now she was in the fucking shower taking all year, saying her pussy was hurting. I was dressed and ready and she still hadn't come out the bathroom.

After 30 minutes of waiting, she walked out the bathroom with just her panties on. She was bowlegged, but she was being extra walking with her legs wide open and shit.

"It ain't that fucking serious, Jhenga. You acting like this our first time fucking." She was annoying as fuck, but I loved her.

"Boy, fuck you, my pussy lips is swollen because you wanted to beat the pussy up instead of going slow. Nah come help me get dressed." She had an attitude, but I ignored it. Today was a good day, and her nasty ass attitude wasn't about to fuck up my energy. She sat on the bed and I put her shoes on first. I put her bra on next then her dress. Her hair was in an abundance of curls, making her face look fat, but I wasn't about to tell her that. She was glowing and beautiful, but any lil' thing about her weight made her fucking cry. She stood and looked in the mirror, and I saw her bottom lip trembling.

"Aye, no tears tonight. This is a beautiful event," I lied, because I didn't know what the fuck was about to happen.

"I love you, Nemesis." She turned around and kissed the fuck outta me. Her tongue slithered in my mouth as I sucked on it. My dick got hard as a rock.

"You must want a nigga to bend you over again." She jumped her ass back and refreshed her lipgloss.

"Nah, I'm good," she said as she walked out the room with me in tow toward our awaiting limo. There would be no driving tonight.

22
ZULU

"Damn, Zubae, that's my spot," Haze moaned as I stroked her deep from behind. I grabbed the back of her neck, pulling her to me. We were supposed to be getting ready for this ceremony shit, but when she came out the shower soaking wet, I couldn't resist. What started out as me eating her pussy and doing 69 turned into a full-fledged fuck session. I didn't give a fuck if we were late. My brothers knew me too well. Sweat glistened on her back as mine dripped on her, and I fell on side of her. Our clothes were already laid out. All we had to do was shower and put them on. I just had to get some pussy first. She lay sprawled across the bed on her stomach with her face toward mine.

"Are you ready for this?" she asked me, rubbing her finger through my hair.

"Yeah, long as I got you and my brothers with me, I can do anything." I meant that shit. We had already discussed moving to Washington just to get far away from New Orleans. I was game because that's where our main ports were. She could get a job anywhere, that's if she really wanted to.

"We gotta get up, bae. Nemesis and Jhenga are on the way." She kissed my lips. I decided to ride in the limo with them because I didn't know what I was walking into. We hopped up and got into the shower. I ate her pussy while she washed her hair, and it ended up turning into round two before we washed each other and got out.

We quickly got dressed and were downstairs before Nemesis' impatient ass could blow the horn. My baby was sexy as fuck in her red Gucci mini dress and red bottoms. I matched her with my gray suit with a red tie. I had my hair freshly lined and in a bun, because my shit had grown to the middle of my back. I wanted to rip that fucking dress off her, but I had to let my baby do her thing. Lives would be spared tonight because they knew who she belonged to. The rings proved that.

"Oh my god, look at your belly," Haze said looking, at Jhenga's belly.

"Please don't fucking say that, or we'll have to go home to change," Nemesis said with a stern look on his face. I laughed because I knew when Jhenga was mad, hell's gates would open up.

"You look good, bitch," she told Haze as they hugged and began to talk. Nemesis pulled out a blunt and looked at Jhenga for permission.

"I don't care, long as we don't smell like that loud shit when we get there," she said as the limo pulled off and we smoked the blunt.

23
ENDYMION

These niggas were always late. I believed they would be late to their own funeral. We sat in the car with Potato bouncing around, waiting on their limo to pull up.

"There they go," Lady Bug said as I noticed the stretch Hummer pulling up in front the hotel.

This shit looked like a red-carpet event. There were cameramen out front, people waiting for us to get out the car. They even had NOPD and bodyguards holding the crowd back. This really was on some top-level shit. Their limo pulled up behind our truck and we got out. I went to the back seat and grabbed Khenzington, who stole the crowd. Cameras were flashing and reporters were asking us questions, which we ignored. I stood at the truck waiting for Nemesis, Jhenga, Zulu, and Haze to get beside us. We had to show them that we were a unit and nothing could stop us.

"Nigga y'all just had to smoke a fucking blunt before we went in, huh?" I looked at Nemesis and Zulu.

"I don't know about you, but I had to take the fucking edge off," they both said at the same time as the photographer took pictures of us.

We walked the red carpet like the hood royalty we were. A

nigga felt like he was about to receive a fucking Oscar or a daytime Emmy from the way people crowded us. Once we got inside the hotel, security led us to the ballroom, and when the double doors opened, it was like walking into another fucking world. Everything was blue and red like these niggas were crips and bloods. We walked in and I noticed that our table was on the fucking stage. I looked down at Khency because I knew she hated crowds, and she kissed my lips, assuring me that she was okay. We were escorted to the stage and everybody stood as we walked to it. Fucking respect. That act alone let them know they had real niggas in their presence.

Once we were on the stage, we pulled our wives' chairs out for them to sit before taking our seats. Potato sat between us and smiled for the camera. Lady Bug laughed at his antics.

I noticed Magnolia and Zenobia and Jahari and Amerika sitting before us, and Magnolia nodded his head at me. I nodded back and brought my two fingers to my forehead to salute him. Then my eyes met Mahyesha, and she winked then rolled her eyes. I forgot to tell Lady Bug to call her, so she was probably mad. Her mean ass. The waiter came around with appetizers and Khency took the entire platter from him and pushed him away. Her greedy ass caused the entire crowd to laugh. She and my son ate the fried fish until it was all gone. I looked to the left and noticed Meyhani sitting with I'm guessing his wife, and he, too, nodded at me. If this was what a king felt like, then I was definitely ready to take the crown.

24
MEYHANI

Miss Jazzie put me in this part of her book for a reason. Simply because it was the end. I'd watched from afar the way Grela forced her way into those boys' lives, but I always knew they would catch on and end her. I knew all about the situation with their parents, but we couldn't interfere in family business. That was the number one rule for the Masons, leave home at home, but I knew that shit was bound to happen.

Adonis started fucking Grela and got caught up in her web and was injected with her venom. He couldn't live without his wife but couldn't leave Grela alone. Natasha knew about it, but she ignored it until Grela started making her presence known. She made their life hell and Adonis couldn't handle it. I just hated how the shit went down that night. If I could have taken the boys away that night I would have, but it was against the rules. Now they were grown men and about to take over the most powerful crime mob of the United States. They didn't even know the power they were about to possess. I felt like a proud father as they sat on the stage like a happy family. I stood from my seat, and the waiters went to the stage with crowns and tiaras for the family.

"Attention, everyone. Y'all know I'm getting old and shit and I had a good run. Magnolia is doing a hell of a job running the Masons, and I applaud him for pulling through the way he did." I paused and looked from him to the stage.

"I've known these men before they knew themselves, and to be this close to them is truly an honor. I am honored to place the throne on not only one but three kings to take over the Mardi Gras Mafia. Gentlemen, crown your wives and then yourselves."

I raised my glass along with everyone else in the room as they followed instructions. I sat my glass down and clapped my hands as everybody followed, because I had done right by Adonis' kids, even in his death.

25
MAHYESHA

Y'all know this book couldn't end without me popping my shit. You always save the best for last, and I'm the oldest and last motherfucker standing. It hurt me to have to kill one of my best friends, but you gotta remember when to hold and when to fold, and that bitch folded and I had to kill her. I am more than willing to share my love with Khency and her kids because I knew how Grela loved her. Granted, I would never want to replace that snake, but I would love her better than Grela ever could because she's the girl I always wanted but never got.

"What you over here talking about?" I turned around, and it was Khency looking at me with her tiara slightly crooked. I reached my hands up and adjusted her crown because I would be the one to make sure it never tilted again.

"Oh, nothing," I told her as the DJ dropped Beyonce's rendition of 'Before I Let Go."

"Come on, fat momma, come dance with your new mother." I winked at her, and she smiled as I pulled her to the dance floor.

And oh, don't worry, my son and his new brothers and sisters aren't ending yet. Yeah, they got their happy ending, but y'all know Magnolia's walking now, and some shit gon' shake in the next series, only this time he got an army with him.

Bye y'all, but we'll be back though.

ALSO BY MISS JAZZIE

Married To The Don Of New Orleans 2

Married To The Don Of New Orleans One

A Nolia Boss Saved Me

A Nolia Boss Saved Me 2

A Nolia Boss Saved Me 3

www.ingramcontent.com/pod-product-compliance
Ingram Content Group UK Ltd.
Pitfield, Milton Keynes, MK11 3LW, UK
UKHW040042200726
13854UKWH00001B/499

9 798757 199764